The Perfect Gift

Mark Stewart

The Perfect Gift

Mark Stewart

Published by Mark Stewart, 2023.

This is a work of fiction. Similarities to real people, places, or events are entirely coincidental.

THE PERFECT GIFT

First edition. December 17, 2023.

Copyright © 2023 Mark Stewart.

ISBN: 979-8223492221

Written by Mark Stewart.

DEDICATION

I'd like to dedicate my novel 'The Perfect Gift'
to my wife and family for putting up with the 400 hours
I spent writing the book.

THE PERFECT GIFT

CONTENTS

by mark stewart
Fire games
Heart of a spider
I know your secret
Kiss on the bridge
Kiss on the bridge two
Kiss on the bridge three
The perfect gift
Blood red rose
Blood red rose two
Blood red rose three
Legendary Blue Diamond
Legendary Blue Diamond two
Legendary Blue Diamond three
Planet X91 series
Don't Tell My Secret
201 May Street
The Girl from Emerald Hill
Ladies' Club
Mistress
Book of secrets

CHAPTER ONE

A YOUNG man boasting a straight back, used deliberate steps to march up to the open casket. For a long moment, he stared at the dead woman lying in the coffin. Eventually, he lifted his gaze and looked at the small group who had come together to pay their last respects. The young man's expression portrayed someone who seemed detached, totally uninterested. His actions dictated the fact he wanted to be somewhere else.

The young man slowly returned his attention back to the viewing. He leaned over, staring closely at the old woman. Her face showed no sign of any anguish she may have encountered throughout her lifetime; her stories gone forever.

A middle-aged woman, fresh tears cascading down over her cheeks, followed slowly in the man's footsteps. She stood next to him speaking in low whispers.

"Why did you come?"

"I needed to see for myself." His voice sounded full of scorn, bordering on hatred.

"I repeat my question."

"Don't talk to me. In a few minutes, I'll be gone, never to return." He squared himself to the young lady and looked directly at her eyes. "You'll never have to see or hear from me again."

"That suits me fine."

An old man, leaning heavily on a walking stick, shuffled forward. Standing between the two, he whispered. "Not here, not now."

"Who are you to tell me what to do?" grumbled the young man. He glared cruel eyes at the old man.

"Jake, can't you speak nicely?"

"Shut up Bernice. I'll speak anyway I want."

"You shouldn't have come; there's nothing for you here."

"I'll be the judge."

"I hope you didn't come for money?" questioned Bernice.

"There is no need for you to know the reason why I came."

Bernice bowed her head, sobbing quietly. She hugged the book she held tighter. "I refuse to fight with my only brother."

"At last, you're starting to see things my way. I choose what I want and when to do it."

Bernice stared at her brother. "Your black suit matches the color of your nature. Here, before you go, read this. You owe it to mother," she insisted, shoving the book at him.

"I owe her nothing. I warned her not to stay at the Oasis. She didn't listen."

Jake snatched the dull red leather-bound book from his sister and threw it on to the floor next to the coffin. He marched past the onlookers to the outside.

Bernice picked up the book. She studied the expensive cover for damage. With a long sigh, she held it tight. Stepping into the sunlight, Bernice glared at her brother, lighting a cigarette.

"I see you're into a healthy lifestyle."

"What's it to you? Why do you even care?"

"I know you should've given mother and father a chance before turning your back on them and the Oasis."

"Poppycock! I decided I didn't want to live in a prison."

"I have never viewed the Oasis as a prison."

"It's high time you did."

"How can I? I have always loved the place." Bernice, again shoved the book at him.

"What's the book?" snarled Jake.

"Every one of mother's thoughts is recorded in the book."

"In her memoirs," corrected Jake. Pulling off his tie, he shrugged a shoulder.

"Why don't you read the book for five minutes?" urged Bernice. The sparkle in her eyes forced Jake to hesitate.

The old man who stood at the coffin emerged from the graveyard quiet funeral chapel. He stood on the top step, grinning. His furrowed brow depicted he'd seen too much sun over his lifetime.

"Stop smirking," yelled Jake, lifting his fist into the air. "Old man, if you want to fight, I'm ready."

"Come, sit in the privacy of the quiet room overlooking the grounds," hinted Bernice, stepping in his way.

"The only destination I'm interested in is the local hotel for a drink."

Bernice cleared her throat. "Please, we have much to discuss." A soft, pleasant expression swept her face. Her tone of voice could melt the heart of any man.

Jake slipped out of his pinstriped suit jacket and dropped it over his arm. "I'll give you five minutes; not a second longer."

Bernice pointed to a narrow path, leading through the manicured garden to another building not far from the chapel. She climbed the steps and waited for Jake to catch up. When they entered the building and walked into the small room, she closed the door.

Leather bound law books each one in mint condition filled the bookcase adjacent to the door. A Tasmanian oak table and three chairs were set up in front of the window. The grey carpet looked new.

"Sit down. I want you to read the first page," jeered Bernice, shoving the leather-bound book under his nose.

"What if I don't want to sit?"

"I insist." Her soft, gentle voice, her feminine facial expression, she left on the other side of the door. The tone in her voice now sounded cold, almost hostile.

Jake pulled a second cigarette from his pocket, placing it in his mouth.

Bernice reached out, yanked it from between his lips and threw it in the small bin next to the table. "You can't smoke in here," she scolded.

"Don't tell me what to do. I need something to settle my nerves. I don't like it here. I want this day to be over so I can get back to the city. It's where I belong. If you stopped to analyze what I just told you for five minutes, you'd know I'm correct."

"Is that the reason why you smoke?"

"What I do is none of your business."

"I suppose that was a fair comment."

"I'm thrilled to the back teeth; we finally agree on a second idea."

"Brother, even though we don't get along, I'm happy you decided to be here. Your presence means a lot to me."

Jake answered in a flat voice. "I'm thrilled to be here."

"Why do you have to be so cynical?"

"I've told you this before. It's my business, not yours."

Bernice's shoulders slumped. She looked away to hide her tears.

"What did you expect?" queried Jake.

"Couldn't you have visited me and our parents at the Oasis at least once in the last twenty years?"

"Tell me, who in their right mind would want to visit the Oasis? The place isn't exciting. In fact, it's an isolated, boring hole in the ground."

Bernice again stared at her brother. "It's a lovely place. If you'd only given it the chance it deserves you might have found it therapeutic. If you had stayed for a week, you would never want to leave."

"Spare me the grief. It's a boring, horrible place. I grew up there just like you."

"We had great times waiting for the leaves to fall off the trees so we could kick them high in the air. Not to mention saying what we thought a cloud resembled or what it might change into as it floated past us."

"If you say," said Jake, interrupting. "I used to dream every night about leaving the dry, dusty forsaken land. When I left, I never looked back." Glaring at his sister, he dropped the book Bernice gave him on to the desktop. "If you had followed me, you'd feel the same way I do now. The city's nightlife made me rich. The city itself is exciting beyond belief."

Bernice carefully picked up the book. Forcibly she pushed it against Jake's chest. "Read it. You owe the dead woman. If you've forgotten who she is, the woman was your mother. Her name was Naomi."

"Again, I tell you I owe her nothing." Jake glanced at the waste paper bin and lobbed the book through the air. It missed the bin, landing heavily on the floor.

"Maybe missing the bin was an omen," hinted Bernice.

Jake retrieved the book from the carpet. His second attempt successfully ended with the book in the bin.

Bernice folded her arms. She looked down her nose at her brother through cold, unfriendly eyes. "If what I am about to say are the last words, I tell you then so be it. The city, the money, will never replace the splendor of the Oasis which is located in the middle of the Australian outback. Nothing compares to the morning glory that fringes the white clouds every new day, the birds, the cattle, or the peace the place brings."

"Forget the wise old words. Tell me one thing before I leave. The old man hobbling up to the coffin, who was he? Did you know him? He resembled the local street bum."

"He's no street bum. He came to say a few last words and to relive old memories." Bernice walked over, picking the book out of the bin. She cut into the path of her brother, marching for the door. "Sit down and read." Again, she shoved it at his ribs forcing him to hold the book.

"Tell me one good reason why I should read it?"

"I have already told you the book contained mum's entire memories."

"I do not care," Jake looked at the book then at the bin. He made preparations to lob the book high over his siter's head.

"You should care."

"Out there in the middle of Australia, she was never a mother to me. I'm happy I left home at an early age. The city helped me grow up."

The door to the room opened. A man wearing a two-piece grey suit and a white tie hanging from his neck walked in.

"Excuse me, Sir, is your name Jake Stanton?"

"Who wants to know?"

"I'm the solicitor in charge of the family fortune."

"Go away; you're not needed."

"Sir, the book you are holding has been left to you in the dead woman's will."

Jake massaged his temples. "What is it about this stupid book?"

The solicitor lowered his voice, the tone changing from friendly to authoritative.

"Before the reading of the will commences, you and your sister must read the diary. Failure to heed this simple command will see you both automatically cut from the inheritance."

Jake's deceitful city nature slipped into overdrive. By kicking the chair across the room, he wanted the man to know he wasn't happy. He pointed directly at his sister's green eyes.

"I'll read the first and the last page."

Opening the leather-bound book, Jake commenced reading.

CHAPTER TWO

CLOSE TO the sand in the tranquil Port Phillip Bay, forty minutes from Melbourne, the small church looked picture-perfect. The ten bouquets of freshly picked red roses tied neatly at the end of each pew were exquisite. The flower girl and bride's maids looked superb.

The bride looked out of the long narrow window at the side of the church altar. She watched a brown leaf fall from the large oak tree. She marveled at the way the sea breeze helped it float gently to the ground. The bride-to-be faced her future husband. The expression on her face radiated love and devotion. Her long white silk dress and veil hid her nervousness.

The minister's eyes sparkled. He used a distinct deep tone of voice to close his debut wedding. "Naomi and Bill Prescott, I now pronounce you man and-."

"Hold it. Freeze the wedding service," yelled a young woman standing in the exact center of the main doors leading into the church.

Her words cut deep into Naomi's spirit. She turned away from her future husband and glared at the person who interrupted her day. The one hundred strong onlookers, the same ones who made a ruckus over her four-thousand-dollar wedding dress were gob-smacked.

For far too long the old church remained barren of sound. Naomi's heart skipped a beat. She wondered had the priest heard.

A rude mix of deep and high-pitched verbal diarrhea erupted from the guests. Every eye in the weatherboard building stared at the barefoot woman in a torn sky-blue dress. She stood square to Naomi just inside the main door holding a baby while sweeping a young girl closer to her left hip.

Three kids fanned out from behind her.

Naomi looked at the sullen group. Switching her attention back to her future husband she whispered. "Bill, do you know this woman?" Her voice sounded alarmingly calm.

"I have never seen her in my life," he mumbled.

Naomi watched the woman marching along the pale red carpet. She abruptly stopped at the foot of the altar. The woman glared at each of the bridal party then studied Naomi's wedding dress. Looking directly at Bill, she spat at the slate tiles he stood on.

"Excuse me," said Bill.

"Bigamy is against the law, darling," snarled the woman.

"Excuse me," scoffed Naomi, echoing Bill's remark. "Who are you? What do you want?"

The tall, thin, woman swept long blonde hair from her face. "I'm here to stop this farce of a wedding."

Naomi's best friend and bridesmaid, Kaite, stepped forward, shoving a tight fist at the woman's nose.

"You might want to reconsider your idea," she yelled through a locked jaw. "Leave before this scene turns ugly. You certainly have not been invited."

The woman pointed her finger at Bill. "I can prove I'm this man's wife."

Naomi folded her arms. "Let's see the proof."

Bill started to fidget. He focused on the many guests hoping they weren't about to lynch him. "Yes, let's see this so-called proof."

The woman snatched a photo of Bill and her on their wedding day from the hand of a young sobbing four-year-old girl. The woman shoved the photo and a copy of the marriage license at the priest.

His shocked expression said it all.

#

Naomi was lying prone on the bed staring at a dirty smudge mark on the ceiling. Her arms were folded.

Naomi looked at Kaite who appeared to be busy getting ready to go out to yet another nightclub in Melbourne.

"Kaite, Bill had been an amazing man, the perfect gentleman and easy on the eyes. He didn't have to work too hard to sweep me up into his fantasy world." She sighed, jumped from the bed and walked across the room to the window.

Kaite rolled her eyes. "The falling leaf must've been a bad omen. It's been two years today. Get over it."

"I can't."

"Tell me something, did lover boy pay you any money for ruining your day? The dress cost you an absolute fortune let alone everything else he made you buy."

"No."

"Do you know where he is or what he's doing?"

"No."

"My dear girl, stop moping about this tiny shoe box-size apartment. Let's go out and have some fun. I can already hear the nightlife calling from the Melbourne CBD, and the sun has yet to set."

"I don't feel like doing anything," admitted Naomi on a sigh.

"What about the bloke you met recently? Heard from him lately?"

"Don't even start to mention him. Sometimes I feel he's out there still watching every move I make."

"You never did say much about him," grunted Kaite.

"There's not much to tell. We met on the dance floor three months ago. By the end of the night, I figured him for a creep. I ordered him out of my life."

Kaite looked out across the Melbourne skyline at the setting sun. "You are correct, he did look like a creep. We should go to the local nightclub. I'm positive we will meet someone new."

Naomi lowered her gaze to the street below. The people rushing past their building reminded her of ants. She knew the streetlights were about to blink on. The city's nightlife will soon follow. She loved the dancing, the smell of the countless coffee shops, the restaurants and the theatres. She turned from the window, walked across the room and sat on the end of the bed.

"I've made up my mind, no more men."

Kaite giggled. "Don't make me laugh."

"This time, I'm serious. Men are big trouble. The only thing they want is a quick roll in the hay. When they get bored, they dump me and go searching for the next one. I'm convinced there's not a man anywhere in Australia who cares enough about a woman to treat her like a lady. I've been searching for years hoping to discover a man who is honest and will stay by my side for my entire life."

"You won't get an argument from me. There's only one thing wrong; you will be lonely for the remainder of your life," said Kaite.

Naomi flopped prone on to the bed. "I think I've made myself depressed."

She eventually dragged her feet back to the window, palming an open hand at the city skyline.

"Surely, I'm wrong. There must be a decent man out there somewhere."

"If you quit trying so hard, maybe he might surface. Come on my dear girl, get dressed, the two of us are going out to have a great time and find romance."

CHAPTER THREE

"EXCUSE ME, lady; my name's Brandt. You're in my seat." He reached up, taking hold of an overhead leather strap. He stood swaying slightly to the rocking motion of the train. His facial expression portrayed a little boy who'd lost the most precious thing in the world.

The woman, on the higher side of middle age, didn't look happy. She stared at the man hovering over her. He wore a plain dark grey suit, white shirt, and matching tie.

"Just in case you have any doubts, I sat here first, sonny," she spat.

"I always sit in the seat closest to the front of the carriage."

"Do you really? Since when?"

"Yesterday," announced Brandt.

"Get a life."

"Please, I need to sit in your seat."

"Listen, fella; I can see at least twenty vacant places in this carriage alone."

"I'm asking politely," pleaded Brandt.

"Go away fly. I don't like it when men grovel. They sound pathetic. Deep down they're not real men at all."

A few people diverted their gaze from the fences flashing past the train windows to the man towering over the woman. Whisperings travelled at speed from person to person throughout the carriage. In less than a minute, laughter erupted from the forty commuters.

"I know I'm making a fool of myself, but what if I paid you?"

"Can't you tell I'm not interested?"

Brandt fished for his wallet. "Twenty. I'll be happy if you would accept a twenty-dollar note. The only thing you need to do is vacate your seat."

The lady lifted her hand in an attempt to hide her proud look. She winked at the late teen girl sitting opposite her.

"I will pay you two-hundred for the privilege of sitting in your seat."

The woman looked up. "You must be desperate."

"It's imperative I sit in your seat. I have exactly three minutes remaining."

A tall heavy-set man wearing a black bikie jacket walked the length of the carriage. The man had rolled up his sleeves, revealing a large ugly tattoo of a skull and crossbow on each massive arm.

"Lady, is this bloke annoying you?"

"Yes, he is."

The heavily tattooed man grabbed Brandt by the tie, dragging him in close. "Fella, leave the lady alone. There's a seat with your name on it at the other end of the carriage."

"I need that particular seat she's sitting on," moaned Brandt.

"Give me one good reason why I shouldn't knock your block off?"

"I don't need to give you a reason."

"I'll punch your lights out mate if you don't walk away."

"Please, listen to reason. I offered to pay for the seat," explained Brandt.

"How much?" asked the man.

"This fly offered me two-hundred dollars," the lady explained.

The heavy-set man stared at the woman. "Lady, I'd take the money."

The woman stood, staring directly at Brandt, holding out her hand.

"Thanks for vacating the seat!" Brandt dropped the money on to the palm of her hand and watched the lady walk to the other end of the carriage. He saw her sit, scrutinizing his every move.

When Brandt spied the train which he hoped carried the young lady he'd seen in the nightclub a week earlier starting to draw level, the other commuters watched him staring out of the window. Curiously they focused on the approaching train. Their whispers echoed the same words.

'What's so important?'

The two trains slowly drew level. Brandt couldn't hide his disappointment. He faced the people staring at him.

"When I drove to work the other day, I saw a gorgeous young lady sitting in the other train while I waited at the rail crossing. Except at the nightclub, it's the only other place I've seen her. I did hope to see her close up. She's not sitting where I thought she'd be."

"Try a different window," called the lady he had given the money to. "This scene is more interesting than a TV drama."

Brandt's pupils danced at the hope as he sprinted from window to window. He started to panic when the trains began to drift apart. Staring out of the last window he caught a glimpse of her. The young lady looked up, making a cursory glance his way. She flashed a quick smile just as the trains forked and went their separate ways.

Brandt leapt into the air. He yelled at the top of his lungs. "She looked at me and smiled."

"I too saw a young good lookin' Sheila glance your way, fella," stated the man with the skull and crossbones. "She's a bit of alright. If I, were you, I'd track her down even if it took me all my remaining days. I believe it was worth every cent of the two-hundred bucks you paid just to catch a glimpse."

"I'm off to the office," announced Brandt.

Devin, Brandt's best mate, stumbled out of his bedroom on the way to the kitchen. Focusing on the wall clock, he mumbled. "It's only 6:30 in the morning."

"I want an early start."

"No, you don't, you're obsessed with trying to find the woman you saw last Saturday night at the nightclub and again when you were on the train. You've been tracking her down for the past three weeks."

"I can't get her image out of my mind."

"Heed my advice, give it up," snarled Devon.

"After spending two-hundred hard earned bucks to buy a seat on a train, I'll never give up the chase. She saw me looking at her and she deliberately smiled at me. The two-dozen people I've talked to on four different train stations told me they had seen the girl. I'm more determined than ever to find her."

"Why do such a thing?"

"Do what?"

"Pay two hundred dollars for a seat on a train?"

"I'd pay a thousand dollars just to catch another glimpse of her."

"You're crazy," jeered Devin. "I suppose I'll have to help you. The sooner I do the quicker you'll forget the woman; especially after she tells you to get lost. Maybe then you might listen to me."

"I don't need your help to find the love of my life. I know the train she catches," advised Brandt.

"Let me tell you something. I've heard enough about how you hound each woman you meet. Don't forget, the boss wants us in his office first thing this morning. There's a rumor circulating around the office he's looking to handball an important advertising project to someone. If you're not in the office on time, I won't be making up any excuses."

"Don't worry about me; I'll be there."

Devin shook his head, watching the front door close. After making a mug of coffee, he went back to bed.

Brandt arrived at the train station fifteen minutes before he expected the young lady to appear. He marched over to an old woman selling flowers from under a faded blue awning.

"How much for a bunch of red roses?" he asked.

"For you, fifteen dollars," answered the woman in a strong Italian accent.

Brandt paid the money and got busy watching business people bustling past. Leaning against the wall of the ticket booth, he spied the young lady he'd been searching for walking towards him. Completely hypnotized by her poetic movements, Brandt watched her stroll to the end of the platform. Naomi stood staring down the tracks for the next train when Brandt made his move. Walking up to her he studied the style in her long auburn hair. The clothes she wore reeked of business. She looked tall, thin and ultra gorgeous. Brandt stepped next to the woman, straightening his tie.

"These are for you," he said, thrusting the flowers forward.

The young lady smiled at Brandt. "They're for me?"

Brandt already felt excited. To him, the young lady's voice sounded angelic, the perfect pitch.

"Yes, for you."

"Have we met? You look familiar."

"Sort of," answered Brandt.

"Correct me if I'm wrong; didn't I see you yesterday when our trains were travelling in the same direction? You pressed your face against the glass."

"Yes. I've been searching for you everywhere since I noticed you on the dance floor a few Saturday nights ago. I've even been having dreams about you. Please, don't be alarmed, I've never seen a woman more beautiful. Your eyes, face, clothes, are picture-perfect. May I ask your name?"

"It's illegal to stalk someone," she quipped.

"I know it is. I have to confess you're the most beautiful girl I've ever seen."

"You've already said that compliment. I'm flattered, Mr.?"

"I'm Brandt Dusting. What's your lovely name?"

"Naomi. I stand by what I said about the stalking issue."

"Please, accept my small gift of flowers."

Naomi eyeballed the man suspiciously. "I'm not certain if I should."

Two hundred eyes watched the man grovel as one hundred commuters readied themselves to board the approaching train.

Naomi shot the man an innocent schoolgirl's smile. "Judging by the looks we're receiving; I'll have to accept."

"Thank you."

"No, thank you."

A loud applause erupted from the commuters who were inching closer to the edge of the train platform, waiting for the train to rumble to a stop.

Brandt asked his question over the squeal of the brakes. "May I buy you a coffee sometime?"

Naomi's grin hid the fact she felt deeply embarrassed.

"It's the least I can do seeing how you have made a complete jerk of yourself. I'm always at the office an hour early, now's a good time. If you turn out to be a weirdo, I can leave and still be at work on time."

Brandt followed Naomi into the train carriage, inviting himself to sit next to her on the seat closest to the door.

"What career are you into?" asked Naomi, starting the conversation.

"Advertising for the television. I'm an advertising executive. What about you?"

"I'm not convinced I want to reveal my career at this early stage."

"I live about ten minutes from here. Do you live close by?" asked Brandt.

Naomi focused on his seemingly honest eyes. "I'm close, yes."

"I hope I'm not moving too fast; can I have your phone number?"

"Sure, why not. This station is our stop." Naomi stood and waited for the train's door to open at the platform. A multitude of people bumped the pair as they attempted to step off the train.

Brandt escorted Naomi across the busy road to the coffee shop, opened the door, closing it in his wake. The two ordered their cappuccino and sat in the last two seats furthest from the door waiting for the drinks to arrive.

The café appeared to be quiet. Three other customers sitting at an outside table were drinking their coffee. They seemed oblivious to the fact cars and trucks were cramming the road. The wind created by the many vehicles constantly buffeted a blonde-haired lady's long hair.

"Please inform me if you're single?" asked Brandt.

"Yes, I am. Are you?"

"Yes, I certainly am."

Naomi leaned forward across the table. "You do realize I'm not the girl of your dreams."

"I believe you are."

"You don't know anything about me."

"At the moment, I don't. There's no doubt in my mind I want to."

They swiped their mug of coffee from the hands of a smiling late teen boy and fell silent waiting for the lad to walk off. Naomi felt uncomfortable at the overbearing man staring at her and turned her head to look out the window at the people walking past on their way to work.

"I'm positive when you discover I'm a nice bloke, I know you'll want me in your life," advised Brandt, reaching out to hold Naomi's hand.

"I'll see what the weather brings. Hopefully, it won't rain."

"Can I buy you lunch?"

"Okay, you seem like a nice enough bloke. You can pick me up outside the court house at twelve noon."

"You're a lawyer?"

"Sort of. I work for the taxation department. In two hours, I have to be in court to testify someone had committed fraud."

"Sounds like an exciting career. May I sit at the back of the court? We can walk out together."

"I think it'll be nice if you were there. It's been a tough case."

Naomi could feel her heart starting to melt. Maybe there was a slim chance the man sitting opposite her was indeed the decent bloke she'd been searching for.

Brandt conjured up a meaningful smile, slipping his hand around Naomi's.

"May I walk you to the courthouse?"

"I think I'd like that." Naomi gathered up her bag and briefcase and followed Brandt out of the cafe.

CHAPTER FOUR

"YOUR HONOR, the witness has stated he'd been drinking heavily on the night of the alleged fraud and the disappearance of Mrs. Annette Craven. I believe the witness' statement has been soiled," insisted Naomi.

"Objection your Honor, we have already established my client consumed no more than three drinks," bellowed a tall heavy-set man wearing a black Italian suit.

"Where's this leading to?" asked the Judge. "The court has already heard all this."

"Your Honor, I'm attempting to discredit what the witness, Mr. Johnson, is telling us," stated Naomi.

The Judge made a flippant hand gesture. "Get to the point."

"At 1:00am on Tuesday the eighth of November 2005, Mr. Johnson's statement reads, and I quote his exact words. 'I saw the accused, Mr. Luke Craven deliberately and with a degree of accuracy, displaying a determined expression on his face walk across the room, sit opposite a man and commenced to write out a cheque for five thousand Australian dollars.' Is this statement of yours, correct?"

"Yes."

"How close were you to the scene?"

"About ten metres," said Johnson.

"Your statement reads; 'you followed the man who you have stated was Mr. Luke Craven to his home and hit a man over the head using a beer bottle. You then drove the victim to the hospital.' Is this correct?"

"No."

"It's your statement to the police," growled Naomi, throwing the paper she held at his face.

"I'm confused," mumbled Johnson. He started drumming his fingertips together.

"You're confused due to the fact you witnessed nothing. Luke Craven paid you so he could have an airtight fraudulent alibi. There was no attacker; no beer bottle for you to use as a weapon. Your Honor, this farce has gone on long enough. This so-called witness is, in fact, nothing more than a hired man who has been paid to lie to this court. Summing up, I have proof; two airline tickets were purchased; both are a one-way trip to England, one for Mr. Craven and one for Mrs. Craven."

"Objection," yelled the other lawyer.

"Over-ruled," advised the Judge.

"Okay," yelled the man. He pounded the desktop using a tight fist. He stood and pointed a stubby finger directly at Naomi.

The security guard grabbed his arm, forcing him to sit.

"Craven had swindled millions of dollars from a lot of people and devised a way to protect his wealth while keeping them off his back. He asked me to help him fake his death. If I agreed he'd pay me a million dollars. He signed over everything he owned into his wife's name. Four weeks after his funeral I was to buy an airline ticket to England. When I arrived, he'd hand over a further five percent of his cash. It's a mere pittance of the amount in his Swiss bank account. He didn't know I wanted everything. His cars, his mansions, his summer home in Hawaii and his entire Swiss bank account containing thirty million dollars. To top it off, I had planned to make Craven's fake death real. His passing would give me the green light so his wife, Kianna, and I could have a great life together. We've been secretly seeing each other for over ten years."

The Judge stared at the man. "Case closed. Arrest the witness. I will also send a message to the police to arrest Luke Craven and his wife."

The gavel came down ending the court case. The large room erupted into a loud ruckus. The media personnel spewed out of the building towards their news van. Each wanted to be the first to report on the case.

"You were awesome. Naomi, behind your beauty is a clever mind," boasted Brandt. He waited patiently while she packed her black leather attaché case.

"Thanks for the compliment."

"Lunch?" asked Brandt.

"I want to take a walk first. The walls have ears in a café." Naomi looked directly at Brandt's eyes. "Please, don't take the idea of a walk the wrong way. After the courtroom fiasco, I'm a little drained. I always take a walk after a legal battle. You're more than welcome to join me."

Brandt and Naomi strolled across the road, entering the Melbourne botanical gardens. The path appeared to be weed free. The smell of freshly cut grass still hovered in the air.

"If you have a problem, I'm here to listen," hinted Brandt.

"Thank you. If I may be blunt, I'm concerned about moving into a new relationship."

"I think you have a case of cold feet."

"I believe it's something more."

"Why?"

"The last man I loved turned out to be a bigamist. I discovered the ugly news standing at the altar in my wedding dress the day before my twenty-fourth birthday."

"I'd never do anything so horrible. I believe a woman should be admired. She needs to be treated affectionately at all times."

Brandt ushered Naomi along the path towards a garden seat situated under a large gum tree. A young couple walking in a loving embrace glanced at them. Brandt displayed an angry stare. His expression didn't alter until he saw the couple scurry off towards the road. Brandt waited for Naomi to sit on the wooden seat then mirrored her posture. He held her hand. Naomi felt uncomfortable over his unsolicited move. She pulled her hand away after she waited patiently for an elderly couple to shuffle past.

"Enough about my background. Tell me what you're working on?" asked Naomi.

"I have to think up a slogan for hair shampoo."

"How's it coming?"

"Great. Want to hear it?"

"Okay."

"I based the slogan on someone I know."

"Who is the person?"

"You."

"We don't know anything about each other."

"We don't have to. The minute I saw you on the dance floor you stirred my imagination. The slogan is still untitled, though I'm thinking along the lines of; 'To catch your mate in seconds.' The entire advertisement will run something like this. 'Two trains come together. The girl looks up when a man in the other train notices the shine in her hair. He sets out to find her. Eventually, they get married. The actors will say a punch line something like the following; using this shampoo, men will notice you even when you're on another train.'

"Corny," advised Naomi.

"What do you mean?"

"I think our time together is over."

"I can't allow it," demanded Brandt.

"Please respect my wishes when I tell you I never want to see you again."

"You can't walk out of my life. You're my soul mate."

"I certainly am not," grumbled Naomi. She stood, hovering over Brandt.

"Please, give me a chance. It's the only thing I ask."

"Thanks again for the flowers." Naomi extended her hand to attempt a business-like handshake. She waited for Brandt to copy.

He never did.

"Do you believe in love at first sight?" asked Brandt.

"No, I don't. There's no such thing."

Naomi retracted her hand, placed her handbag on her shoulder and picked up her briefcase. Brandt watched the woman walk along the solid brick path back towards the road. He stretched and marched after her.

CHAPTER FIVE

"KAITE, DO you think I could be mistaken for a man in this outfit I'm wearing?"

Naomi's best friend stared at her with doubt written in her grey eyes.

"Comparing your figure to a man's, no matter how hard you try you'll never resemble a bloke. I wish I could have a figure just as good. How many times have I said you belong on the catwalk, not in the taxation office, or courtroom?"

Naomi twisted and turned in front of the full-length mirror glued to the door of her bedroom. She had just bought new blue denim straight leg jeans and a pale blue western shirt in a one-hour bargain sale from a small shop not far from the courthouse.

"Are you positive I couldn't pass for a bloke? The mirror depicts otherwise."

"What gives?" Kaite rolled off the bed. She walked over to the full-length mirror.

Naomi's eyes sparkled. "Does my shirt and long auburn hair clash?"

"We've known each other since pre-school. Have I ever lied to you?"

"There has been one time," she giggled.

Kaite poked Naomi in the ribs.

She squealed. "I'm kidding!"

"Tell me the real reason why you want to look like a bloke? I thought you wanted to marry and have a couple of kids?"

"It had been my plan."

"What's changed your mind? Have you and Brandt been fighting again?"

"Yes. He's turned over a different leaf. He's gone from a rich green color to a rotting stinking brown."

"Care to explain?"

"Not only did he turn into an obsessive monster, I asked him what he thought the perfect gift for a woman might be. I'm happy I found out the truth. He only wanted me for two things; a roll in the cot and his stupid advertising slogans."

Kaite pretended to vomit. "A bloke like him, you don't need. How did he answer your question?"

"He believes in his miniature brain a woman only wants plenty of money to spend." Naomi flopped backwards on to the bed.

"You're joking?"

"No. I had hoped he would be Mr. Right. He turned out to be Mr. Wrong. Kaite, I'm fed up. All men lie and cheat. I've given up on thinking a man could ever understand or even contemplate the meaning of the perfect gift."

Naomi walked to her seventh-floor apartment window. She used the back of her hand to part the curtains. With a far-away look in her eyes she stared out across Port Phillip Bay.

It was Halloween 2009.

Twelve months to the day at their first Halloween party, Brandt finally asked for her hand in marriage. He officially announced it on an impersonal level. Everyone she knew received an invite to the party. Her parents, his parents, Kaite, and of course all their friends. She did enjoy the party. Music sounded great. Food tasted terrific. She finally put the embarrassing announcement behind her by convincing herself it must have been his nervous nature. After the party, they sat on the beach watching the full moon slowly sink in the night sky. Sitting on the sand under the stars felt romantic. Falling asleep in each other's arms until the sun came up happened to be a moment she wanted to cherish.

Naomi sighed away her disappointment, studying the lights of the city. She definitely felt passionate over Melbourne's nightlife. She lowered her gaze to the street below, focusing on the cars as they were driven at speed past the building. She then took notice of the people.

They looked the size of ants, hurrying along the street totally unaware someone was watching their every move. From the moment, she and Brandt broke up, she lost the desire to party. She felt lonely to the bone. She wanted to meet an honest man. Brandt came across as a good talker. He respected her at first. He hid his obsessive nature to perfection. Failing to discover the perfect gift quenched her love for him. Could it be there's no such thing? Naomi stared sideways at Kaite.

'If you didn't help me, I'd have never made it through,' she thought.

Focusing on the West Gate Bridge, Naomi watched a ship slowly slip underneath its wide span. She saw several street lights blink on. She smiled at their friendliness. Port Phillip Bay looked inviting. She imagined the long hot days to come when people flocked to the water's edge to escape the Melbourne summer.

"Kaite, somewhere out there a man must be waiting. I wonder if he's lying on his bed looking up at the ceiling thinking where his, 'Miss Right' could be. He might even be wondering what she's doing right now. Or maybe he's being driven in a limo to a nightclub. Maybe he's a pilot preparing to depart for America or London or Jamaica. I want to find a man who is strong, honest and fun. I want him to give me the perfect gift."

Kaite walked across the floor. She draped her arm across Naomi's shoulders. Her free hand scraped the long auburn hair from her face. She leaned sideways and whispered in her ear.

"You're rambling. You must know you won't find a man anywhere in Melbourne, especially at the tax office who has any idea on the perfect gift. I have a strong feeling such a man doesn't exist."

Naomi's pupils sparkled. "I need a change."

"You're scheming something, what is it?"

Naomi walked to her bedside table, opened the top drawer, wrapping her French polished nails around a newspaper article. She marched back to the window, flapping the paper at Kaite's face.

"What's this?" Kaite grabbed the paper before it swung back and hit her in the nose.

"Read the situation vacant column. I want to know what you think?"

Kaite dropped the newspaper article to arm's length. "I thought you told me the tax office is a great place to work. You love the job."

"I do. I love all those numbers. I live to work. I want to work to live," explained Naomi.

"If you love the job so much what's the problem?"

"It's like you said, Mr. Right doesn't work in Melbourne."

"You want to throw in the towel after two bad relationships?" questioned Kaite.

"I want to work where Brandt has no hope of finding me. I need to feel safe from his obsessive nature."

Kaite read the job advert. "You're going to work as a waitress on a cruise ship?"

"No. My plans don't include water. You know I can't swim. Read the article underneath."

Kaite dropped her gaze back on to the paper. "You've underlined the next job advertisement." She threw the newspaper on to the bed. "The job sounds a little too drastic a change."

"It'll be perfect," chirped Naomi.

"You won't find any decent men out in the middle of nowhere."

"Out in the Australian bush there are no beaches to drown in either," stated Naomi.

"Mightn't be much water; what about the number of snakes you will see?"

"I love your baby python."

"There are other varieties out there. Need I remind you; one bite and you will be dead in minutes."

"I'll be fine, thanks for asking."

"What about the notion you love the action of the city?"

"The job's only for two weeks. Besides, it gives me an opportunity to forget Brandt. I need time to clear my head. It'll give me a much-needed rest. Two weeks of not thinking about a man who only wants me for his job or a roll in the cot is exactly what I need."

Kaite looked down her nose, shaking her head.

"You don't have to scold me." Naomi sounded hurt.

"How long have I told you to move on; to forget the bloke?"

"It seems forever. I felt totally in love. Brandt eventually showed his true leopard spots. I trusted him when he said he had to work late. I even made-up excuses in my mind when I rang his mobile phone and Gina, his secretary answered. What makes me choke is the fact I discovered he took her to the place we called ours. That was where we enjoyed our first all night date and I gave him my heart. He called the place a sacred site. He knew how much I loved it. He wined and dined her in the Chinese restaurant then escorted her upstairs. Why take her to the restaurant where we first kissed? Every year on our wedding anniversary we were going to book our room. It happened to be a beautiful place overlooking the bay. An opened bottle of champagne in an ice bucket in the middle of a small round wooden coffee table wrapped up the scene. What upsets me the most, they slept together in the same room, the same bed we did. He promised to take me back to our room each year to celebrate our anniversary."

"Don't start the tears again," warned Kaite.

Tears cascaded down Naomi's cheeks. Her voice began to falter. "He broke my heart. How I would love to cut him up into little pieces and feed him to your pet python."

"Get over it. You found out about the other women six months ago."

"I intend to forget all about Brandt. I vow from this day forth I will not give my heart to another loser. I will never make the same mistake again. I'm going to search for Mr. Right. If he can't figure out what the perfect gift is, he can ride his bike into someone else's life. I can guarantee she won't stick around for long."

"Good luck. I've been searching for years to discover the right bloke."

"If I stay positive, surely the right bloke will enter my life."

"This job mightn't be exactly what you have interpreted," hinted Kaite, changing the subject. "Why don't you look for a city job? There are a lot of nightclubs we haven't been to yet. Or you could always take me to Perth. My bags are packed."

Naomi dried her eyes. She swiped the article from off the bed.

"I'm twenty-six. I'm in need of a holiday. The interview is tomorrow morning."

Kaite snatched the paper out of Naomi's hand. "The advert states; a man going by the name of Mr. Earl Stanton is searching for a Jackaroo."

"Read on," urged Naomi, sounding excited.

Kaite dug her nose from the paper. "They want a bloke who has knowledge of office duties."

"The add states not essential."

"You're overlooking one important fact."

"What?"

"This Stanton character is looking for a bloke."

Naomi shrugged, diving into the wardrobe for a small suitcase. Her voice came back muffled. "I'll be a Jillaroo."

Sitting on the bed, Kaite read more of the article aloud. "You have to be at Moorabbin airport no later than 6:00am. Naomi, you don't get out of bed before 7:00am."

CHAPTER SIX

AT EXACTLY 5:00am Naomi arrived at Moorabbin airport by taxi. The scene reminded her of an old horror movie where the cop had followed the murderer to an abandoned warehouse. The only thing missing was the fog.

The taxi driver looked at Naomi in the rear-view mirror. "Excuse me, Miss, the office, forty feet from where I have stopped is your destination."

"Thank you."

Naomi leaned forward and paid the fare. She collected her suitcase from the trunk and watched the taxi as it was driven towards the main entrance to the airport.

Then the tail lights were gone.

Alone in the cold and dark, Naomi studied her surrounds. She spied several light planes anchored to the ground with ropes and the airport's control tower appeared abandoned.

The word 'mistake' filled her mind. Naomi folded her arms in an attempt to stay warm.

"This place is only forty-five minutes from the Melbourne CBD. My enthusiasm has waned," she mumbled, trying to rub the goosebumps from the surface of her arms.

'Maybe Kaite was correct. There is no one here,' she thought.

With the strap of her knapsack draped over her shoulder and the small suitcase in tow, Naomi lifted her head, squared her shoulders under the sudden weight and walked to the closest office block.

After trying to open the locked door to the first office, Naomi looked through the window into the dark interior. She felt the cool breeze sweep her cheeks. The clang of something metal against the flagpole around the other side of the building caught her attention.

The clanging sounded intermittent at best. Naomi decided to investigate. She walked around the corner of the building and spied three flagpoles. A floodlight poured light on to a narrow concrete path. A twin-engine plane sparkled in the security lighting. Naomi marveled at its near new condition. Then she saw the large square box with holes in the sides on the ground near the plane's front wheel.

'Obviously, someone is loading the plane,' Naomi thought. She stepped into the shadow of the building and watched.

The idea of smugglers or just plain illegal goings on stirred her imagination. Naomi reached for her mobile phone, her index finger hovering above the number zero. Three quick jabs will have the cops listening to any illegal jargon she might uncover.

"Bad idea. The light from my mobile phone could easily give away my hiding place."

Naomi slipped her mobile phone back into her jeans pocket and slid along the building's wall, praying the large box on the ground belonged to Earl Stanton.

The distance between the office door and the tip of plane's wing couldn't have been any more than several large steps. Standing next to the opened office door and hearing nothing, Naomi looked in. A single 60-watt incandescent light globe lit the deserted internal office space that looked no larger than a small shed. Naomi entered and dropped her bags on to the grey carpet. Her reflection in a small square mirror hanging on the wall watched her every move. Naomi noted the wrinkles on her brow made her look nervous. She had dressed in the dark so as not to wake Kaite. Naomi pulled a hair tie from her top pocket and quickly tied her hair into a tight ponytail. Watching her shoulders slump, she faked a grin at the mirror.

The image in the mirror did the same.

"This is a stupid idea." Remembering the vow, she told Kaite, the image in the mirror wagged a finger at her. "I can do this. I'll run the outback farm using an iron fist. I'll show those farm boys who the boss is, even if it's only for two weeks. Look out boys Naomi Fitzgerald is on her way. Goodbye Brandt, you heart breaker."

Naomi heard a cough. She turned on her toes and faced the office door. The man casually leaning against the doorframe seemed content in watching her. His six-foot two-inch frame took up most of the space. He wore faded blue jeans and a white-collar shirt. His handsome, tanned face seemed to grin at her. His azure-colored eyes glistened from the overhead light globe.

"Can I help you, Miss. Fitzgerald?"

"You can, yes."

"Are you a movie star?" asked the man.

"No, I'm not. Why do you ask?"

"Movie stars talk to mirrors. I thought you were rehearsing some lines to a smash hit production."

"You watch too many movies," mocked Naomi.

"I don't watch any movies, including westerns."

Naomi saw the man's natural smile deepen. She'd never seen a more provocative smile on a man. It seemed to reach out to her, saying, come and get me. Her body tingled at the thought of falling asleep in his arms under a million stars on a clear night. She sighed inwardly. 'What a fantasy.'

"What do you do in your spare time?"

The man began to chuckle.

"I don't think my question was all that funny!" jeered Naomi, folding her arms.

"Wearing your type of outfit, I felt positive you'd be staring in a western movie."

"You sound like a jerk. Believe me; I've known a few in my time."

"Is there anyone in particular?"

Naomi scoffed at hearing the question.

"Don't turn defensive on me; I'm only making conversation."

"My personal life is none of your business."

The man stepped into the office and walked towards the filing cabinet at the wall opposite the door.

"Stay away," warned Naomi.

"I've been given permission to be in here. Have you?"

"If you're Mr. Stanton, yes I have."

The mystery man looked Naomi up and down. He raised his eyebrows. "Did you buy a new outfit?"

"If you're so hooked on what a person wears you should take a look at yourself sometime."

The man fell silent staring at his short-sleeved white-collar shirt, faded blue jeans and dirty boots.

"Did I scratch an open wound? I must advise you a coiled length of rope clipped to your brown belt doesn't help you to look fashionable. Your oversized brass buckle could use a good polish."

"My family is in a little financial trouble."

Naomi's face took on a touch of crimson. "I'm sorry."

"I'm attempting to say you'd look great wearing anything, even if you had to borrow my dirty belt for a while."

"If you're trying to apologize, I accept." Naomi pointed to his belt buckle. "What's the inscription read?"

"Read?"

"What's the word on your dirty brass buckle?" Naomi questioned.

"Oasis," answered the man.

The corners of Naomi's mouth quivered slightly. Remember your vow, she warned inwardly. No man will try to run your life again. She successfully painted a picture of Brandt in her mind so she could display a heartless stare at the man. She couldn't tell if he had tried to make a pass at her or soften her up for a surprise attack.

The man opened the filing cabinet and rummaged through a drawer full of papers. He eventually found a notepad, closed the drawer and brushed past her on the way to the table.

Naomi frowned at the touch of their arm. His skin felt hard from a lifetime in the sun. His shoulders were square and solid. She decided the man had seen a lot of hard work over the years. Standing in front of him she cast a shadow over the page he started writing on.

"Are you still here?" he asked, looking up.

"Yes, I'm still here. I'm waiting on information. Do you know Earl Stanton? If you do, where can I find him?"

Naomi felt her knees buckle at seeing the man's natural smile again. She groped for the table's edge.

The man stood, reaching out his hand. "I don't think you're about to jump me. I'm Trent."

"Naomi," she said.

They shook hands.

"Naomi Fitzgerald, yes, I heard you say your name to the mirror. What makes a beautiful girl come here at this time? I'm sure you didn't come here to talk to yourself in a mirror." Trent started to chuckle yet again.

"Do you think it's funny?"

"Not on the least, sweetheart."

"I'm not your sweetheart. Tell me, why were you laughing?"

"You, being so gorgeous, I thought you were a movie star."

Naomi gagged on her next breath. His sentence took her by surprise. She felt angry at hearing the flattering words. She felt frustrated and embarrassed at the same time. She couldn't remember a time when a man didn't throw himself at her.

"I've already stated why I'm here. How many different ways do I have to say I'm looking for Earl Stanton?" Naomi pulled the neatly folded newspaper add out of her top pocket, dropping it on Trent's notepad.

"I don't think you are the right person for the job," he argued.

Naomi leaned on the table. She easily resisted the urge to kiss the man. Whether Stanton felt happy or not he was going to give her this two-week job. "How do you know?" she hissed.

"I just know."

"Tell me where Stanton is? I want to hear his argument myself."

"He's at the Oasis."

"It doesn't make sense. The article in the newspaper states I have to be here at 5:00am. Now you're telling me he's at a place I've never heard of."

"Lady, don't waste my time. I have a lot of work to do, and not much time to do it. I want to depart for my home in five minutes."

"Where is home?"

"I'm not saying."

"Or you won't say?"

Trent stepped over to the filing cabinet, locked it then walked towards the office door.

"I gave up sleep to be here at this lousy time of night, the least you can do is tell me where I can find Stanton?"

Trent shrugged, stepping out into the cool air. He raised his shirt collar as he walked towards the plane. Naomi watched him push the large box gently into the plane and close the cargo door.

"Is Stanton in another building?" Naomi asked, marching over.

Trent looked at Naomi. "You sure are a stubborn woman."

"I am not. I'm a determined one."

"He's not anywhere around here. He's at the Oasis."

"Yes, you've said. If you'd be kind enough to point me in the direction of this, 'Oasis place,' you keep referring to, I'll be on my way. We'll never see each other again."

Trent pointed towards the north.

"Thank you," jeered Naomi.

In the sudden temperature drop of the new day, Naomi rubbed her bare arms. Retrieving her bags from the office, she displayed a sour expression.

"Are you planning to walk there?" asked Trent. He let go of another slight chuckle.

"I don't think it's any of your business." Naomi picked up her bags and prepared to walk off.

"Now look who's being pig-headed?"

"How far is it to the Oasis?" Naomi questioned.

"Four hours."

"I can handle a four-hour walk."

"Four hours of flying time. I'm about to depart for the Oasis. After I've made a quick phone call and provided, the boss says okay, I'll take you there; deal?"

"It's a deal."

Naomi watched Trent study the sky for a long time. She saw him shake his head then look at his watch.

"Is there something wrong?" Naomi tried hard to use a caring voice. It sounded the opposite.

"Maybe," he mumbled.

"The word 'maybe' isn't a proper answer."

Trent grabbed Naomi's bags. He placed them on the ground next to the plane, snatched his faded brown leather jacket from inside the plane, handing it over. "Here, put this on, you look cold."

Naomi felt grateful for the gesture, slipping into the oversized jacket. She wondered how Trent could tell in the half dark she felt cold. Or in fact, why should he even care?

"The old thing looks better on you than me!" exclaimed Trent.

Naomi grinned, trying to convince herself the knocking of her knees was caused by the cold and not from the smell of his manly after-shave trapped in the jacket's collar.

"Miss Fitzgerald, are you okay?"

Looking at Trent's handsome, tanned face made her feel worse. "Yes. Why?"

"Your face looks a different shade. I'll make my phone call. It won't take long."

Naomi shook her head to ward off the impulses raging through her body. She mustered every ounce of willpower to avoid jumping at Trent. 'I'm just a sucker for a pilot.' She fumed at her thoughts. Her knees caused her legs to turn to jelly. She needed to sit. Finally, Naomi gathered some decorum.

"It must be the cold," she croaked.

Taking Naomi by the hand, Trent led her back into the office. He gestured at a seat in the corner near the door, placed her bags on the floor and helped her to sit.

Naomi sat looking directly at his striking deep blue eyes. 'Don't you dare lose it, girl,' she ordered inwardly. 'Control yourself. Remember your vow to Kaite. No man will ever again ruin your life. Discovering the perfect gift is the only way she'd ever change her thinking and allow a man into her life.'

"I'm concerned about the weather," announced Trent through the phone. "I'll be back on time if the fog doesn't roll in."

"Time?" Naomi echoed the word louder than she wanted. She didn't like people listening in on her private conversations. She inadvertently found herself doing the same.

Trent glared at Naomi. Raising his finger to his lips, his friendly eyes looked cold. "I detest people echoing my words."

Naomi decided not saying another word might be the best course of action.

Trent nodded a few times at the phone, mumbled the word okay then slipped the mobile phone back into his jeans pocket. His friendly expression quickly returned. "I mentioned to Mr. Stanton we'll arrive on time if the fog doesn't ground us."

"Is it a bad thing?"

"Girl, what planet are you living on?"

Naomi clenched her fists and folded her arms.

Trent raised his hands. "We have to get back to the Oasis ASAP. Those letters mean as soon as possible."

"I know what ASAP means."

"Good to hear."

Naomi began her summary starting with Trent. Obviously, the man wasn't a beer slurping, gut aching, two-timing rat like Brandt. He looked tall, dark and handsome. He resembled someone you'd only read about in a romance novel. His friendly dark wind-swept face could easily melt any lady he came into contact with. She focused on his black hair and blue eyes. Trent locked his gaze on Naomi. He grinned. She grinned back. He chuckled. Naomi echoed the sound. She wanted Trent to take her in his arms, melting his lips against hers. She quickly started to fantasize about how his lips might taste.

The shrill of the man's mobile phone interrupted Naomi's erotic thoughts. Trent stepped away a few metres, pulling the phone from his pocket.

Naomi studied the photos on the wall. There were three prints. Each depicted the same B52 bomber taken from various angles.

Trent caught Naomi's attention when he looked up. She easily picked up shreds of the conversation. He pointed to her a few times before slipping the phone back into his pocket.

"Are you going to let me in on the conversation?"

"No." Trent marched out of the office and into the pre-dawn mist.

"You don't have to be so blunt about it," Naomi stated.

She followed the man to the twin-engine Piper Cherokee. Her knowledge of planes was sketchy at best. Her father owned a restricted license. On her sixteenth birthday, her father took her up for a sky tour of Melbourne. He piloted a plane similar to this one on that day. Happy birthday, she remembered him singing. Three weeks later while her father drove towards Moorabbin airport, he died by the hands of a drunk driver. Naomi turned her head away when a tear rolled down her cheek.

Trent stepped to her side. "Are you okay?"

To Naomi, the tone of his voice seemed to float on air. She stared directly at him. Instead of Trent's face, she saw only her father's. She missed his gentle words and the way he laughed. Her mother kept to herself after the accident. Finally, after refusing any help, she took her own life two months after Naomi turned twenty-three. Thanks to Kaite, she had enjoyed life. They could be found at a different pub every Saturday night. At times, Naomi wanted to drink her life away. Eventually, she and Bill were drawn together which ended in disaster at the altar. Soon after that horrid day, she met Brandt. She shook her head. He happened to be sweet at the beginning. As she fell in love, he started changing. He'd stay away from her for days on end; when he came home, he smelt like a perfume bottle. He explained it away by insisting he bought her an expensive bottle of perfume which leaked over everything. His excuse only washed the first time. Kaite talked her into following him for a few days. They both took several days off work and discovered him in the arms of another woman. Naomi sighed. She so desperately needed to unburden her horrible memories of Brandt.

Trent casually waved his hand in front of her face. "Earth to Naomi Fitzgerald, are you okay?"

She shook her head, glaring. "Shut up," she whined.

"Excuse me?"

Naomi back stepped away from Trent. She felt drawn to him in a way she never expected. It wasn't his fault her life ended up in a mess.

"We have to get going," urged Trent.

"I thought you said we'd be grounded due to the fog?"

"I did."

"You lied. I don't like liars."

"I didn't lie. Plans have changed since making the decision to wait for the fog to lift. If we leave now, we'll be okay. I've been in touch with the Oasis. They gave me instructions to wait five more minutes for any stragglers to arrive."

"Stragglers?" questioned Naomi.

"Anyone who might turn up hoping to snag a two-week job," explained Trent.

Naomi glanced around at the empty airport. "No one else seems to be arriving."

"You're it. You do realize the job is only for two weeks?"

"I only want to stay for two weeks."

Trent grunted, studying her clothes. "By the look of you, I'll be amazed if you last two days."

Naomi stared the man down. "Want a bet?"

"What have you to offer?"

"When you lose, we have to dance together in front of two witnesses," advised Naomi. "You're too large to know how to dance."

"If I win, you have to kiss me before I fly you back here."

"Sounds like a fair bet," said Naomi.

They shook hands to concrete a gentleman's agreement.

"If you are employed as a pilot who runs errands for Mr. Stanton, tell me how you know so much about this job I'm taking? Stanton seems to have a lot of faith in you."

"I know the Stanton's very well. They trust my judgment."

Trent locked the office door. Picking up Naomi's luggage he led the way to the plane's door. Placing her bags into the plane, he waited patiently for Naomi to climb onboard. When she looked seated, he locked the side door. While Naomi buckled her seat belt, Trent slipped into the pilot's seat. He reached out, flicking the ignition switch to the 'ON' position. The blades of both engines slowly rotated. Inside a minute, the plane was stationary at the end of the runway. The occupants of the plane sat in the dark listening to the drone of the two engines building up speed.

CHAPTER SEVEN

THE FOG easily consumed the plane as it motored along the runway. The buildings changed to a blur. The airport's control tower came and went. It resembled a tall structure straight out of a black and white horror movie. Naomi still couldn't see a single light anywhere or a friendly wave by someone who came to watch the plane take off.

Naomi stared into the white void hoping to be the first one to see the arrival of another plane. She watched Trent who looked to be concentrating. She watched him volley his gaze between the fog and the tarmac several times. The plane tilted upwards. The white void quickly turned wet. The moisture thickened the higher the plane ascended. Finally, the fog started to disperse at the three-thousand-foot mark.

At five-thousand feet, Trent leveled the plane. Naomi craned her neck to look out the window. She saw a blanket of white below them. The sky in front of the plane looked to be an expanse of pale blue.

"I have a couple of questions," she said.

Trent flashed her a cursory glance then re-focused on the sky ahead of the plane. "I'm listening."

"Did you consider waiting for the control tower to give you permission to take off?"

"No."

"Tell me, did you contemplate any danger in taking off in the fog?"

Trent didn't answer. He remained preoccupied in studying the plane's compass. He slowly moved the wheel forcing the plane to sweep gently to the left. He reached out switching on the autopilot. He glanced at Naomi's green eyes.

"I made a calculated accent."

"Calculated?"

"Yes."

"You were guessing, hoping we didn't crash into another plane?"

"Not exactly," Trent answered.

"Explain it to me." Naomi folded her arms to show she wasn't happy. It entered her mind how this so-called expert pilot could be so blasé with their safety.

"I talked to the control tower yesterday morning after landing. They informed me of the weather. They said there might an excellent chance of fog by 5:00am. They also informed me no planes were due to arrive at the airport before 8:00am this morning. They added the tower won't be manned until 7:00am. To answer your question, my calculated risk was extremely low."

"Why did we have to rush to get air-born?"

"It's raining where we are going."

"I'm not scared of a little rain, are you?"

"No, I'm not scared either." Trent backed up his short sentence with a sharp chuckle.

"You're a mysterious person," moaned Naomi.

"I want to keep a low profile," said Trent.

"You don't talk much either."

"I only talk when I've something important to say."

"You love the idea I know nothing about you."

"Yes, I do," said Trent.

"I'm asking you to let me into your world."

"Why?"

Fantasy thoughts were tumbling through Naomi's mind as if they were in a washing machine. She suddenly realized she regretted the bet they made. It could have at least waited until tomorrow.

"What on earth are you thinking about?" asked Trent, grinning at the woman's faraway expression.

"My thoughts are private. They certainly don't concern you unless you tell me about yourself."

"I'll pass," said Trent.

Naomi stared out of the window on her side of the plane flabbergasted at seeing the land underneath them.

"I'll always be amazed at how big Australia is," she commented. Looking at Trent, she felt surprised he appeared not to be interested in the surrounding view or an ounce of concern at the approaching rain. "How many hours will it take to get to this Oasis place?"

"Three and a half hours."

"Do we have enough fuel?"

"Yes. We'll make it by a good twenty minutes."

Naomi nodded, agreeing the information sounded correct. "Now might be a great time to get to know one another."

"Do you think?"

"Yes."

Trent raised an eyebrow. "Ever seen morning glory at five thousand feet?"

"I've never heard of the name."

Naomi felt torn between attacking Trent due to his handsome looks and accusing him of deception. How could she even contemplate a relationship with the man? He certainly didn't come across as the relationship lasting type. He never did prove Stanton lived at the Oasis or if they were flying in the right direction. For all, she knew he could be taking her for a ride on a one-way ticket to nowhere.

Minutes slowly ticked off. Naomi felt stupid. She knew nothing about Trent, yet here she sat, in a plane, shoulder to shoulder, totally trusting a stranger. She started to be suspicious of the man. Could this be a trap to lure females into a place where the only way out was to jump. She looked out the small plane's window at the five-thousand-foot drop.

"You're not planning to jump?" asked Trent.

Naomi wiped her stare from the window. How could he have known what she'd been thinking?

"The thought never entered my mind. Is there a reason why you asked?"

Trent shrugged his shoulder. "If you look due East, you'll see golden edged clouds. The phenomenon has a name."

"Morning glory?" guessed Naomi.

"It's a beautiful sight."

Gluing her gaze on Trent, Naomi used her peripheral vision to look. How could she have gotten into the plane? At least sitting in a car, she could jump out. She started to wonder if this man who calls himself Trent could actually be on the level.

Trent reached out, grabbing her knee.

Naomi screamed, jumping in her seat. This was the moment she dreaded. She had made it too easy for him. How could she be so naive? "Leave me alone."

"Sorry, I didn't mean to startle you."

"Don't touch me."

Naomi squirmed in the seat. She tried to lean towards the window, but her seat belt forced her to stay exactly where she sat.

"I won't bite. I'm only after your attention."

"I bet you were."

Trent shook his head. "You were looking towards the north. You have to look in an easterly direction if you want to enjoy morning glory," he whimpered.

"You're playing a game at my expense, aren't you? I believe you're enjoying every minute of it. The only thing you want to do is take advantage of me."

"Pardon?" asked Trent, a puzzled expression etched on his face.

"Don't pardon me, mister."

"I do find you easy on the eyes."

"You're only buttering me up so you can win the bet."

"Nothing could be further from the truth. If you want to see morning glory, look now."

Trent pointed out his side of the window. Naomi looked down his finger. Her mouth fell open at what she saw. Golden edged white clouds dotted the sky.

As the plane slowly ascended, Naomi watched the clouds disperse, leaving a green haze in the sky.

"I don't understand the color," she whispered, almost breathless.

"The green haze is evaporating water," explained Trent. "You see it a lot out here." He leaned close to Naomi, placing his strong hand on her knee. "Miss Fitzgerald, I'm not a bad person. You can trust me."

'How can I trust you?' she thought. 'I've been emotionally scarred by Bill and Brandt. He'd been the biggest liar of the two men. He only wanted me for his advertising campaigns or to be used as his puppet. Now I feel I'm being pulled towards you. How can I trust you when you're not prepared to answer any of my personal questions? What are you hiding?'

Naomi's mind and body ached for the man sitting shoulder to shoulder next to her. If nothing else, she felt clear on the fact she must win the bet no matter what. To win, she needed to squash any feelings she felt for the man. Somehow, she must protect her heart from ever feeling hurt again. She couldn't cope going down the heartache Boulevard for the third time.

The plane leveled at five and a half thousand feet. Stretching to the horizon Naomi saw a flat desert like land.

"Australia sure is a large country," mumbled Naomi. She looked at the ground through a clear section of sky. "How does anyone survive out here?"

"Although the land looks barren, you can survive. Soon you'll discover the Oasis is perfect."

"Tell me about the Oasis."

Trent's face showed a distant look. He sighed. "She's beautiful, full of life. She's such a magnificent place to live."

"Out here where nothing seems alive. I don't understand."

"You will. Want to pilot the plane?"

"You love changing the subject." Naomi fidgeted in her seat with excitement.

"I'm a shy person."

"You're a man who is full of mysteries," cut in Naomi.

"Are you ready for a flying lesson?"

"I am, yes. Before you begin to teach me, tell me something about yourself?"

"Why should I? You are only here for two weeks. What's the point?"

Naomi looked out of the window on her side of the plane. Now she knew his secret. He felt lonely. Why lose your heart to anyone who came into your life for only two-weeks? She turned from the window and looked at Trent.

"I'm ready to take the controls," she screeched abruptly.

"Use two hands."

Naomi held the wheel on her side of the plane in a death grip.

"The plane's yours." Trent tapped her white knuckles. "Stay relaxed. No need to strangle the wheel."

"You're a bit testy."

"Sorry."

Naomi relaxed a little by straightening her back and sitting deeper into the seat.

Trent relinquished control, retracting his hands. "There you go. You are now flying the plane."

"This isn't so hard."

Trent pushed his seat back, lifted his feet, letting them lean on the door handle. He closed his eyes and appeared to be a man who felt completely relaxed.

"What are you doing?" Naomi's eyes were wide. Her words came as a staggered scream.

"Going to sleep," he yawned.

"You can't. How can you trust me? What if something happens?"

"You'll be fine."

"What happens if we arrive at the Oasis while you're asleep?"

Trent looked at his watch and the fuel gauge. "We won't need to start our decent for sixty-five minutes." He closed his eyes and folded his arms.

Naomi reached over, tapping him on the shoulder. Trent didn't move. 'Surely, he can't be asleep already,' she thought. Naomi tugged at his shirt sleeve. Her right hand moved forcing the plane's wheel to rotate violently down. Her face took on a look of terror. She quickly corrected the wheel. Straightening her back, Naomi gazed at the plane's instruments. They were flying level, and the plane hadn't changed direction. It didn't tilt to the side or do anything except stay level. She jerked the wheel to the left then to the right. The plane remained level.

Naomi could feel her blood pressure rise. Her face turned the color of beetroot. "What have you done?" she spat.

With his eyes closed, Trent chuckled.

"I thought you told me I could fly the plane?"

"Are you always this feisty?"

"Men, I dislike the lot of you."

"All?"

Naomi made a fist and thrust her white knuckles at Trent's friendly face. "Yes, all."

He chuckled again, reached out his hand, kissing her white knuckles.

"Don't," Naomi yelped.

"Why not?" asked Trent.

"I don't like it," she snarled.

"Do you want to enlighten me?"

"No. Drop the subject."

"The plane is on autopilot," Trent admitted.

"You're acting like a complete jerk."

Trent lowered his gaze to his feet. "I apologize. If you smile, I'll take the plane off auto. You can have a real fly."

"How do I know you won't try to trick me? I'm not into tricks."

"What are you in to?"

"I don't think I should say."

Trent displayed a scolded expression.

Naomi giggled. "I'm into watching romantic movies while sitting by an open fire."

"Don't all women think the same?"

"Maybe," whispered Naomi.

"What's your favorite dream?" asked Trent.

"Dream?" echoed Naomi.

"Where do you see yourself in ten, twenty years from now?"

Naomi exhaled a huge sigh. "My dream is to meet a man who is honest. He needs to love me for me. After making love under the stars, I want to fall asleep with his arms wrapped around me. I hope my dream comes true before I have aged ten years. What about you? What's your biggest dream?"

Trent's faraway look made Naomi squirm in her seat.

"I want to meet a lovely lady whom I can spend the remainder of my life with. I also want to find a way to save the Oasis."

"You won't meet too many ladies out in the middle of Australia."

"I've met a few. They come out from the big smoke from time to time. Then they leave."

Naomi felt devastated and looked away. She wanted to be the lady of Trent's dreams; however, she could never contemplate moving from the city to the Australian outback. How could she expect Trent to move to the city? Her lungs deflated causing her shoulders to slump.

"Could you ever consent in moving to the city?" she questioned.

"I could never leave the Oasis."

Trent's voice sounded adamant. For a few uncomfortable moments, the only noise in the plane came from the engines.

"If I have to go to the big smoke to find my partner, I will," he admitted.

Naomi watched Trent looking at her. Could he be playing games again? Stringing her along, or could he be on the level? She felt a smile forming on her face. Maybe there's a flicker of hope, a small flame which if given a chance to grow could turn into a raging fire. To hide her grin, she looked away.

Trent's hand brushed against Naomi's knee when he leaned sideways. This time, she didn't utter a word.

"Ready?"

"Ready for what?" asked Naomi.

"To fly the plane." Trent flicked the autopilot's toggle switch to the 'off' position. "You have the controls."

Naomi moved the wheel slightly to the right. She squealed in delight as the plane started to bank. She quickly brought the plane back to level, glancing at Trent. "This is a wonderful feeling. I didn't know flying a plane could be so enjoyable. Thank you for the privilege."

"You're welcome."

The radio crackled in their headset. Trent flicked another toggle switch, enabling the voice to boom in Naomi's ears.

"Oasis to Victor Charlie Foxtrot, four; do you copy?"

Trent raised a handheld mike to his mouth, winking at Naomi.

"Victor Charlie Foxtrot Four to Oasis, I hear you, crystal clear. What's the problem, over?"

"What's your ETA? Have you more than one package? over."

"I've only the one package. I'll be landing in forty-seven minutes; over."

In the long pause, Naomi watched Trent staring at an imaginative fixed object directly ahead of the plane at the horizon. His eyebrows slowly angled to a point.

Naomi leaned towards him causing the plane to change direction two degrees. "What's the problem?" she whispered, quickly bringing the plane back to level.

Trent hunched his shoulders, displaying a blank stare. Reaching out, he flicked the toggle switch back to autopilot.

Naomi hid her disappointment. 'Trent is not just handsome, he certainly knew his way around the cockpit of this plane,' she thought. Naomi allowed her shoulders to slouch, thankful to be able to relax. Watching Trent looking out of the side window again studying the landscape, Naomi noted his eyes were wide. She followed his gaze wondering what might have spooked him.

At first, she saw only white clouds dotting the sky. She failed to notice the white clouds were quickly joining to form a solid front. In seconds, the white front started to change to black.

Trent spoke in a serious tone. "Have to get moving." He leaned forward, turning the autopilot off. He wrapped his strong stubby fingers around the plane's throttle, pushing the lever to its stop.

Naomi heard the plane's twin engines rev to an almost fever pitch.

"Oasis to Victor Charlie Foxtrot, Four," came the same male voice through both their headset. "Move your arse. It's raining buckets over the Oasis. You've got forty minutes to bed the plane."

"The throttle is already fully open," said Trent, through the radio.

"Son, you might have to make the package push, over and out."

Trent chuckled for the first time in five minutes.

"What does the voice mean you have to bed the plane? What's this, 'son,' statement?"

"There's nothing to worry about," said Trent, ignoring her questions.

"Are we running out of time? Are we late for dinner or something? Is our fuel low?"

"No. Though dinner might be late if we don't hurry."

"You're not making any sense. I thought outback people weren't afraid of anything. Surely, you're not scared of water falling from the sky?"

"The voice over the radio belonged to Mr. Stanton. He informed me we need to hurry."

"I take it I'm the only package?"

"Yes, you are, and I'm not about to make you push."

"You're a smart mouth jerk. Why didn't you tell me you're Stanton's son?"

"I don't want to draw attention to myself. Every time I meet a woman, especially a beautiful one, they start behaving like someone they're not."

"Other ladies?" questioned Naomi. She frowned at the jealous feeling starting to grow in the pit of her stomach. For all, she knew Trent might only be an outback clown in a rodeo who could fly a plane. She hurriedly pushed the thought from her mind.

"There's the echo again," mentioned Trent.

"Sorry, I don't understand."

"My father, Earl Stanton is a well-known business man. He's into cows. He has the best breeding stock in Australia. There's also a rumor floating around there's gold underneath the Oasis. He's been visited by many well-known celebrities over the years. Every one of them said they'd buy the place. Dad has never agreed. He never will."

"Who started the rumor?"

"My great grandfather," explained Trent.

"Is there any gold under the ground?"

"No, at least I don't think so."

"What about the other ladies you spoke of?"

"I think I hear a slight case of jealousy in your voice."

"You couldn't have, I don't know you well enough."

Trent put his hands up. "Okay. In case there is, you deserve to know more about me."

"Finally," whispered Naomi. "I didn't want to win the bet we made by default."

The plane suddenly dived then swayed from side to side.

Naomi screamed. Her hands gripped the arms of the co-pilot's chair in a death grip. She screamed again.

"We're okay," comforted Trent, leveling the plane at the fifteen-hundred-foot mark. He slowly descended a further five hundred feet.

"How can you stay calm, we nearly crashed!"

"We were never in danger. We flew through some turbulence. By the look of the sky, it's already raining this side of the Oasis."

Trembling from head to feet, Naomi rolled her eyes. She squinted in the bright sunshine.

"There's not a cloud in the sky out my window," she stated.

Trent tapped her shoulder. She jumped, whirling around to face him.

"See the band of grey clouds directly ahead, near the horizon?" His voice sounded friendly, yet full of authority.

Naomi squinted against the bright sun streaming through the window. She hid her skepticism.

"If you study the horizon to my left, you'll see a solid mass of midnight black clouds," reported Trent.

"I saw them a while ago. The clouds don't seem much of a threat seeing how they aren't directly in front of the plane."

The plane changed direction twenty-seven degrees to the left and started to descend. Naomi's eyes widened, staring at the black mass approaching, now directly in front.

"Tell me you're only trying to scare me?"

"I'm not that cruel. They're bad storm clouds," advised Trent.

Naomi choked on her words. "Why did you change direction?"

"The Oasis is to our left, exactly where the clouds are the darkest."

"Will there be lightning?"

Trent nodded as he made the plane dive towards the ground.

"We're almost there. The wind is picking up. In three minutes, we'll be standing on the ground."

Naomi managed to flash a wintry day smile, watching the clouds loom closer. The black swirling mass appeared to be moving incredibly fast. The clouds resembled large cotton balls which were dipped in black ink and hung low in the sky. Lightning lit the shortened horizon. Visibility plummeted. Naomi felt like a tiny insect that could be easily squashed at any time.

Clutching her seat, Naomi swallowed the lump in her throat. She watched the ground coming up to greet them. What should have been inviting; looked desolate. Every tree appeared dead. The wind swept the ground at speed. Naomi marveled at the dust storm about to swallow the plane.

Trent navigated the plane low over a large square shaped dam then lined up the plane with the middle of a dirt road. Weeds grew right up to its edge. Large dry balls of bracken tumbled across their path in the strengthening wind.

"I hope you're up for some hard work?" questioned Trent.

"Yes, of course," replied Naomi, squaring her shoulders.

The plane bounced a few times on the hardened clay road. When it slowed to walking pace, Trent steered towards a small dilapidated cottage. The thought of giving up, allowing Trent to win the bet flashed into Naomi's consciousness. She didn't have enough time to gather her wits before Trent opened the plane's door, yelling over the noise of the wind, encouraging her to hurry.

The plane came to a stop not more than thirty feet from an old two-room cottage. Naomi scrunched her nose at the broken steps leading up to the main door. Someone tried unsuccessfully to fix a wooden board in front of the broken glass window. Glancing at Trent, Naomi wondered why he had let the Oasis fall apart, seeing how he admitted he adored the place. She didn't understand why he thought the Oasis was perfect.

Naomi decided bush folk and city people thought differently on what were sustainable lodgings.

'Oasis, home sweet home,' she thought. 'If anyone could live in this place, out here in the middle of, who knows where, she could.'

Naomi stepped down from the plane, digging her heels into a dry weed. She felt determined the adventure will be nothing more than a two-week working holiday. She looked at Trent and wondered if he could live in the city, 'big smoke' as he put it, or could he be stringing her along so that he'd win the bet. The bet she would make certain she won.

Naomi clamped her hands together, walking towards the front door of the house. Overhead the black clouds billowed. The first thunderclap rumbled above the noise of the wind.

"Where are you going?" called Trent.

"Inside. I don't want to get wet. Looking at the state of the house, it will take hours to plug each hole." Naomi stood on the first rotten wooden step looking over her shoulder at the man staring at her.

"There's no time; we have too much work to do outside."

"I bet there's more work to be done on the inside. The house probably hasn't had a woman's touch in fifty years."

Trent broke out into a deep belly laugh.

Naomi fumed inwardly at being laughed at. She marched back to the plane.

"What's so funny?"

"I can tell you think this place is the Oasis."

The deep pitch of Trent's voice sounded calming. He placed his hand on Naomi's shoulder. His hard-callous hand sent electricity throughout Naomi's body. Focusing on the house, she began to doubt if the dwelling could even be fit to live in.

"If this place isn't the Oasis, where are we?"

Trent looked seriously at Naomi's green eyes. "This land is part of the Oasis. Where we live is fifty miles further on. We needed to land here to check the fences of the property, the water pump and drop off some food for the hungry gang when they arrive."

"Hungry gang out here?" Naomi craned her neck trying to see through the swirling dust. "I don't see anything or anyone?"

"Come, I'll show you around the place while we start our check."

"Shouldn't you close the plane's cargo door?" questioned Naomi. "I don't want to see you get upset when sand or rain pours in."

Trent looked back at the plane. "It'll be okay, the door's facing away from the wind."

Naomi walked next to Trent. He seemed oblivious to the wind slamming grains of dirt into their exposed arms and face. Using her hands to shield her eyes against the flying dust, Naomi struggled to keep up.

"In seven days, the five acres in front of us will be full of cattle," explained Trent, waving a palmed hand at the windswept clay. "One hundred cows to be exact. The trucks will roll up and the cattle will be loaded. We will sprint for the Oasis and bring the next one hundred cows. We'll keep doing it until every cow has gone." Trent changed direction, power walking towards the dam.

"It sounds like you're getting rid of all your cows?" puffed Naomi, trotting to keep up.

"We are."

"Why?"

"I've already mentioned my family is in a tight financial spot. It's why my father needs an extra hand for the next two weeks. He did hope to have five blokes turn up at the airport."

Naomi stopped. She stared at the back of Trent's head. Tears welled up in her eyes. She bore the resemblance of a woman who'd been overtaken by grief. For the first time, she thought everything she'd gone through might have been on the level. In the sudden lull in the wind, she sprinted towards Trent.

A rogue gust of wind hit Trent square in his face. He lost his balance and fell into Naomi. They both wrapped their arms around the other to stop the wind from pushing them into the dirt. For a long moment, they stood there, in the wind, staring at each other's eyes. Trent leaned his face close. Naomi copied, tilting her head. His warm breath swept her cheeks, fanned by the wind. Their bear hug tightened.

"This is a strange place to start a romance."

Trent raised his eyebrows. Their lips brushed. Naomi closed her eyes, wanting to melt into the moment.

The surging wind pushed both of them off balance. Naomi fell backwards. She closed her eyes waiting to feel the hard ground. She felt no pain when she heard the dull thud. Opening her eyes, she saw Trent's grotesque face. He'd managed to twist underneath to cushion her fall.

"Are you okay?" she questioned.

"I'll be fine if you kiss me."

Naomi lifted her torso off Trent only to be pulled back down. She felt a prisoner in his strong arms. Trent craned his neck. Naomi lowered her head. In the middle of a storm, in the middle of the Australian outback, miles from anywhere, she felt something amazing beginning to happen.

Lightning pierced the charcoal-colored sky. The deep thunderclap lagged behind by only a few seconds. Naomi didn't care. Love started to germinate. She wanted time to speed up so the urges she felt might quickly grow.

"You only want to win the bet."

Naomi had said the words to start to test Trent's honesty. She needed to discover his secrets long before love could even begin to strengthen. If she ever fell in love, yet again, she needed to be fully persuaded. The missing fact must be the perfect gift. If Trent couldn't discover the meaning, she knew love could never stand a chance.

"Forget the bet," whispered Trent. "I surrender."

"I'm not sure you're too convincing."

Trent pushed Naomi off and gently lowered her to the ground. He stood, holding out his hand.

"It's urgent we begin work," he said.

Naomi exhaled away her disappointment, knowing full well the moment was gone. She wondered if the way she felt could be a mistake. She reached out, allowing Trent to pull her to a standing position. Almost immediately the wind tried to knock her over. She lost balance, tightening her grip. Trent leaned into the wind, pulling hard. Instantly she fell back into his outstretched arms. The electricity arcing between them felt hard to resist. Surely Trent felt it too? In her mind, Naomi cursed the stupid childish bet they'd made. It seemed to be getting in the way, causing a stumbling block between them.

The strengthening wind pushed them closer again. The thin sliver of light between them abruptly vanished.

Naomi gagged on the dust in her mouth. "Trent, about our bet," she started.

"You want to back out? Renegotiate?"

This was an awkward time and certainly the wrong place to bring up the subject. One of them must be brave enough to be the first to say. Naomi must be strong for the seed of love to grow. Kaite's father used to say the same thing. Be brave she heard him say over and over. To let a shy person, know how you feel, you must be brave. Take the initiative. Be first. The worst thing they might say is no. Naomi cleared her dry throat by swallowing a few grains of dirt.

"I've been thinking."

Trent looked at the sky, shaking his head. "The storm isn't about to wait. We can talk later."

"I have something I need to say."

"It'll have to wait. The storm is approaching fast. We don't have much time."

Naomi watched Trent march off into the wind. She felt how she looked, devastated. He had conveyed the answer to her question on how he may feel about a long-term relationship. Who was she kidding? She came to the outback wanting to forget about men and how much they hurt her, and here she stood making, goo-gah eyes at a man she barely knew hoping he might be Mr. Right. Her eyes narrowed to slits. Fortunately, she discovered quickly he's definitely Mr. Wrong.

Naomi yelled into the wind. "Trent, you can take your good looks, your masculinity and go back to your cows. In two weeks, I'm out of here."

"Did you say something?" he called from the edge of her sight.

Naomi marched up to him, raising her fist. "Men," she bellowed.

Trent didn't understand her comment. Grabbing her hand, he shrugged.

Together they struggled against the wind in silence. Naomi fumed on the inside. She certainly didn't care less about anything Trent might want to say. Showing her around this God forsaken outback place concreted her thoughts into leaving in two weeks. Not once will she ever give Trent a second thought.

"Workaholic," she whispered behind his back.

The area comprised of dirt and dried weeds. To their left on top of a small rise, a windmill whirled around in the wind, pumping water at speed into the dam. Overhead, a circling eagle flew away.

"What are you thinking?"

"The Oasis, is it like this place?" Naomi yelled.

Trent reached out his hand, patting an escaping curl on the side of her head.

"Don't," she ordered, pushing his hand away. "It's a bad hair day, and..."

"What?" he asked.

Naomi lowered her gaze to her feet. For a short time, she stared at the dirt. "I want out of the bet," she insisted. Her shoulders sagged slightly when she heard the words she'd only been thinking. They sounded dry, almost hostile. She wanted to run away. She didn't want to hear Trent's remarks to her request. Besides, making a bet with a stranger was totally stupid.

Trent lifted his hand to pat the rogue curl again.

Naomi stiffened at his gentle touch. She felt torn between pushing his hand away again and smiling at his thoughtfulness.

"I love your wind-blown locks. I also love the way your long hair would cascade over your shoulders and glisten in the sun if it weren't tied back." Trent reached out to pull at Naomi's hair tie, allowing her hair to fall. "See, I knew it."

Naomi watched his eyes soaking up the look as her hair fell over her shoulders. She rudely pushed his hand away. The look he displayed betrayed how he felt. She wondered how he could be so callous if he weren't at least interested in her. Reaching up, she slipped her fingers through his black hair, pulling him in close. Trent squinted as she felt warm liquid ooze over her fingers.

Naomi wailed, pulling her hand away. "You're bleeding!"

Trent grabbed her hand. He gently closed her fingers one at a time. Bowing his head, he kissed her knuckles. "It's okay. I'm tough."

"You're hurt. You have to let me take a look."

"Later."

Trent and Naomi cringed when lightning lit the sky. A deep rumble quickly followed.

"Why are you so stubborn?"

"There's no time. We have to be going. Besides, I believe you are trying to put me off guard about the bet."

"Have you planned to get me off guard, hoping I'll surrender which in turn will make you win the bet?" Taking a step back, Naomi frowned. 'Don't you dare look hurt,' she screamed inwardly. 'I'm here for two weeks. The minute I win the bet, I'm going back to the city, to my office, to my desk and when I get home, I'm going to forget you and this desolate place. How dare you look at me through big seductive eyes? I've seen the same look too many times. I totally gave my heart to Brandt. He tore it in half.'

Turning on her toes, Naomi marched off towards the plane.

When Trent caught up, he grabbed her by the arm. "I'm sorry if I've offended you."

"Don't, you have work to do?" she hinted, pulling her hand away.

"We do, yes." Trent stepped up to the plane's small cargo door and started unloading the plane. He looked up. "I need you to help."

Naomi stood square to her employer. In silence, they finished unloading the plane.

The wind speed seemed to be increasing towards cyclone strength. Naomi felt the first drops of rain on her bare arms. She couldn't believe the sky could get any darker.

A lightning bolt hit the ground not far from the plane. Following close behind came the familiar deep low rumble. Naomi's eyes widened. She felt a tingle travel down her spine from the warmth of the lightning bolt. She screamed in fear.

"Apology accepted," Naomi puffed, wiping the sweat from her face. "Do we have to spend a lot more time out in this storm?"

"If we hurry, we'll be inside the house by the time the rain turns into a downpour."

"Hurry to do what?"

"We have to walk the fence line."

"Why? It is about to rain." Following Trent, Naomi decided it might be an initiation test.

The next rumble of thunder nearly deafened her.

Trent looked at the dark swirling clouds overhead. "I agree with your idea. It's about to rain. We have to move faster. The quicker we check the fence the sooner we can get inside the house."

Trent forced Naomi to stop every few minutes. He taught her what to look for when she tugged on the fence wire. Naomi studied the landscape, watching the wind sweeping across the dust dry topsoil at full tilt. The few weeds managing to survive in the dry conditions were bending, almost touching the ground. The airborne soil stung her face, burying grains of dirt in her hair. A large drop of rain fell on the bridge of her nose. Naomi looked to the heavens. A drop of water hit her between her eyes.

"Trent, it's starting to rain."

He looked skywards, grabbing her hand "We've no time to waste."

Naomi felt tired walking in the gale force wind and wanted to pull her hand away from Trent's strong grip. Hearing the reverberating throb of the windmill whirring around at speed, she decided Trent would have to drag her along. The water being pumped up out of the ground looked to have already half-filled the dam. The strengthening wind started wobbling the wire fence, creating a high-pitched howl. Naomi looked back at the shrinking house through slits. She spat dirt. Cupping a hand around her mouth, she yelled over the noise of the wind.

"I think the storm's going to beat us to the finish line. Do you want to stop and check the remainder of the fence tomorrow?"

"No. We can check the wire fence while we jog," yelled Trent.

Naomi watched his shrinking form. "Easy for you to say," she groaned, starting to trot.

The wind lashed her jeans, forcing her to walk time and again. It didn't take long before she could barely make out Trent's image through the swirling dust. She watched him stop, pull at the fence and run off again. Naomi stumbled over a weed, falling face first into the dirt. She groped for the fence and grimaced in pain. She felt warm red liquid trickling along her arm. Struggling to a half standing position, she looked up hoping Trent saw her fall. The swirling dust was the only thing she could see.

Double lightning bolts lit the sky directly above her.

"The sun's long gone." Naomi counted the seconds waiting for the thunder. "Three. The storm is only three kilometers away."

Naomi watched another round of lightning split the sky. Again, the thunder boomed. She hugged the ground when the next round of lightning hit a dead tree about forty metres from the windmill.

"Two kilometers," she rasped.

Naomi felt defeated. She knelt in the middle of the dry outback paddock and started to cry. Her tears created dirty streaks over the surface of her cheeks. Slowly she lifted her head, searching the land. Through her tears, half closed eyes, rain, and dust, Naomi called for her knight in shining armor.

"Trent, please come back."

In the fading light, the only thing Naomi could see was dirt blowing through the air and the only thing she heard happened to be the wind lashing harder against her shirt. Dust stung every part of her exposed skin. Naomi tilted her head back and looked at the charcoal-colored clouds. The thunder sounded unbelievably louder? Forked lightning again brightened the sky. The desert landscape resembled a picture out of a disaster movie. The dry dust covered land looked to be fast turning into mud.

"Welcome to the desert," she moaned. Dirt instantly filled her mouth. Her hair flapped behind her like a flag in a storm. Puddles of water were beginning to flow together to form small creeks which were gaining momentum as the rain changed to a torrential downpour.

Forked lightning and thunderclaps rolled together. Naomi lifted her hand. She saw blood pouring from the second hole in her arm. A piece of barbed wire had broken off and found a new home in her skin. She yanked the rusty metal splinter out, throwing it to the ground. Lightning split a tree in half fifty metres to her right. Using her arms, she covered her head as the tree crashed to the ground. The heavens rumbled the ground under her feet.

Naomi felt determined to catch Trent to yell a round of verbal abuse. She fumed at each staggered step she took. A single question haunted her mind.

'Why did he abandon her?'

Naomi could barely see through the torrent of rain. She groped for the wire fence hoping her arms might help her feet to move.

At last, her fingers felt the corner fence post. She changed direction. The wind no longer brushed against her face. Instead, it pushed her sideways away from the fence, towards the huge dam in the middle of the landscape. No matter which way she looked at it, if she clung to the fence the dam shouldn't be a problem.

"I'd certainly drown if I fell into the water," she grumbled, her body convulsing at the thought.

Naomi pulled her hair from her mouth. The small victory of changing direction gave her a renewed confidence. She groaned and tried to increase the speed of her slow pace.

Naomi had only walked twenty-seven small steps when she felt tired again. Naomi stopped to wipe the blood from her fingers, managing to scrunch her last tissue over the cut. Over the sound of the wind, she thought she heard a familiar noise. With bloody hands, Naomi shielded her eyes as she searched the land for what made the noise.

At the edge of her vision, she spied a small round light. It appeared to be coming directly towards her. It seemed relentless in its quest to run her down. Naomi squared her shoulders. Her dust caked eyelids strained to stay open, forcing her to squint. Although exhausted from head to feet, she stared at the light. It travelled at speed a metre off the ground. She shifted her focus to a rock near her left foot. Her wet fingers curled around its jagged surface. Taking careful aim, Naomi hurled the rock through the air. When she heard a thud, she frantically searched for another rock.

The small bouncing light never waived from its path.

Naomi's long hair flapped wet, muddy strands in her eyes. Her new jeans and shirt were soaked.

The next rock she unearthed felt heavier. She lifted her arm, concentrating on the perfect throw, waiting patiently for the light to come closer.

The light eventually came to a stop a few metres from her. Naomi dropped the rock at her feet. The familiar chug, chug, chug helped her to paint a weary smile on her face. She felt too tired to know whether to scream, shout, or kiss Trent. She stood in the middle of a storm, soaked to the skin, looking at a grinning man on a motorbike. Her verbal diarrhea could wait for later.

"I believe I'm going your way. Care for a lift, Miss?"

Naomi swung her leg over the seat, grabbing Trent around the waist. Through his rain-soaked shirt, she could feel his washboard abs. She hugged him tighter.

The bike fishtailed along the fence line, back to the house. At full throttle Trent steered the bike into the huge steel shed, stopping at the last second. He killed the light and flicked the bike's ignition switch to the 'off' position.

For a tad longer than a moment, Naomi remained frozen to the seat listening to the wind and the rain. Eventually the lightning and thunder melted her hands away from Trent's waist. Slowly she stepped down from the bike.

"Let's get inside the house. I'll put the kettle on," insisted Trent. He held up a small brass key.

They traipsed mud into the small back room not much larger than a toilet cubicle. Trent closed the outer door blocking out the storm.

For a few seconds, the silence sounded uncomfortable.

Simultaneously Trent opened the inner door and stepped out of his muddy boots. He reached out his hand.

"Surrender your runners and we'll go inside."

Naomi slipped out of her runners, handing them over. Trent placed them upside down on two waist-high poles, in the rain.

"Don't worry about them. They will be clean in no time flat. I call the vertical poles the bush washing machine."

Naomi didn't argue the point. She felt relieved to finally have the extra weight off her aching legs.

Inside the house, she felt shocked at the neatness. No dust, no draft, no water on the floor.

"Nothing except the best for the Stanton folk out here," remarked Trent. "I know the house looks bad on the outside. I've worked hard to make it livable."

"You?" questioned Naomi, displaying a puzzled look.

"My brother and I have worked in this place for six months. You should have seen it before we started. What a mess. My brother helped when he could."

"What about the broken window, the decayed front step?"

"My brother fell through the window when the step broke last week. He fell off the ladder fixing the gutter too. He's okay. It's the reason why the glass is in the plane. I wanted to fix the window before we sold the place." Trent displayed a stern expression. "Our financial problems are not your concern."

Naomi watched Trent walk to the window. She saw him gaze out at the storm. Eventually, he spun on his toes. He marched across the room and entered the kitchen. Naomi heard a generator start up.

"Country living," she mumbled. Slowly she walked around, soaking her mind in the room's décor. "A couple of wooden chairs and a half-broken wooden coffee table. The mantelpiece over the fireplace has seen better days, though the brick chimney still looks in mint condition."

Outside, the wind kept up its howling. Naomi stared through the window, spying her luggage in the rain. She squealed.

Trent came running. "What's wrong?"

"My dry clothes are in the bag. I must have dropped it when we were unloading the plane."

Trent sprinted out into the rain to rescue the wet bags. Back inside the room, he said confidently. "It's okay. I'll start a fire. The heat will dry some of your clothes."

"Thank you."

Trent walked back into the kitchen. When he returned, he carried two steaming mugs of coffee. He sat Naomi in a chair and ordered her to rest.

"Where were you? Why did you leave me alone in the rain?"

"I thought the best thing to do was to sprint along the fence line back to the house. I knew where you were. I also knew you'd be safe until I returned. I apologize. If I didn't insist you walk the fence line, you'd be drier than powder."

Trent took off his soaking, muddy, wet shirt, walked to the front door, pulling it open. In a slick move, he flung his shirt outside on top of another wooden pole.

Naomi's anger melted the moment her eyes feasted on his upper muscular torso. "Let me guess; the poles are your only means of washing?"

"You've guessed it in one."

Trent started to hum as he marched out of the room. On his return, he had an Esky in tow. After opening the plastic lid, he reached in and grabbed two bottles of beer.

"Care to have one?"

Naomi raised her hand. "No thanks."

Trent noticed her bloody hand. He gently turned her arm over.

"It looks bad. I'll fetch the first aid kit and bandage your hand."

Naomi pushed deep into the chair. Every muscle in her body ached. Somehow, she must make sure Trent never found out how exhausted she felt. No matter what, she must keep up.

Naomi closed her eyes. In seconds she fell asleep.

CHAPTER EIGHT

NAOMI PARTLY opened her right eye. For a long time, she stared at the flickering fire. She could feel the warmth of the flames on her face. Slowly she opened her left eye. Tilting her head, she looked around the semi-lit room. Shadows were dancing on the walls. Naomi swept the blanket from off her chin and started to replay the entire day. The office where she met Trent, the plane trip, the storm, the wire fence and a photo flash of Trent's muscular body brought a smile to her lips. Lying on the worn-out couch, she felt alone and vulnerable. Slowly the fog in her mind lifted, revealing her hero had washed and dressed her wounded hand.

Naomi clawed her way to a standing position. The blanket cascaded off her naked shoulders. The white bandage wrapped expertly around her hand showed no evidence of blood. Gently massaging her stiff neck using her un-bandaged hand, she started to move her stiff muscles. Gathering up the blanket, she reached out for the arm of the sofa to support her weight. After steadying herself she could still feel her body swaying. It felt the same as when her father took her on their only fishing trip. The seasick feeling took hours to subside.

A tall, unshaven man with windswept hair, entered the room carrying three wooden logs. He seemed oblivious to the fact Naomi's gaze watched his every move. He walked across the room, dropped two short logs into a metal bucket then placed the third log on the fire. The man stood and nodded at the flames. After turning away from the embers, he stared directly at Naomi.

"Who are you?"

"Whoa, little lady, don't be too startled."

Naomi wrapped the blanket tighter around her. "Where's Trent?"

"He's outside. I'm Henry, Roy Davey's son," he answered, reaching out his hand.

"I'm Naomi Fitzgerald." She shook the man's hand.

"You're from the big smoke, ain't ya?"

Naomi nodded. "Where are you from?"

"I came from across the road. We're neighbors, Trent and me."

"If we aren't at the Oasis, where are we?"

"You're spot on. This ain't the Oasis, girlie."

"Naomi," she growled.

Henry boasted a blank look.

"My name is Naomi."

"Yeah, right. This is the old Peterson place. You sure are a pretty woman. Love the color of ya skin."

Trent walked into the room carrying a mug of freshly made hot coffee. He placed it in Naomi's hand, glaring at Henry.

"You didn't wake my guest?"

"I stayed quieter than a fox stalking the chickens. I'll be gettin' some more firewood."

"Trent, where are my clothes?" whispered Naomi, when Henry walked out of the room.

He pointed to a pile of material in the corner. "Do you remember the storm?"

"Yes of course."

"Do you remember falling asleep and me grabbing you, before you hit the floor?"

"No."

"Don't feel embarrassed, I was the perfect gentleman. I suggested you take off your wet clothes. I also mentioned you should wrap the blanket you're wearing around you."

"Thank you."

Trent walked over to the pile of dry clothes, throwing them at Naomi.

"I hope Henry didn't come on too strong? He's in the market for a wife."

"What about you?"

"Sure, if the right lady ever came across my path."

"Do you want to tell me more about yourself?"

"No."

"Why not? Why are you so secretive? Have you killed someone?"

"Nothing so drastic," replied Trent.

"You can at least tell me why you insist on having a length of coiled rope hanging from your belt?"

"I'm not sure you need to know," hinted Trent, squaring himself to Naomi.

"I think I have the right to know."

Naomi felt as though she'd walked into the middle of a tug of war where her brain was yelling to put the brakes on. Her heart ordered her to get him so he doesn't slip away. After all the tugging, she knew nothing of the man. His history, what he liked in a woman, disliked. The vow she made to Kaite rang warning bells inside her head. She wanted to reach inside her mind and throw them to the wind. Thinking of how much hurt Brandt caused her, Naomi started trembling inside the blanket. In a heartbeat, she decided her brain would win, for now.

"You don't strike me to be a typical Jillaroo." Trent dropped another log on the fire.

"I'm sure of the fact Mr. Stanton's son is not just a pilot."

"Are you positive?" quizzed Trent.

Naomi watched the embers from the dry four-inch-wide log floated upwards. In a few moments, the tiny sparks had been sucked up the chimney and were gone.

"A typical pilot wouldn't land in the middle of nowhere just to check a wire fence. Maybe I'll throw myself at Henry."

Trent raised his hands. "I have to admit I'd treat you a thousand times more loving than he."

Naomi wrapped her arms even tighter around the blanket. Her heart pounded. The drumming was telling her to jump at the man. She wanted desperately to follow what her heart ordered. Unless she threw herself at Trent, how else could she show him how she felt? If she came on too strong, would he still be interested? Her body erupted in goosebumps, comparing Trent's loving, caring nature to Brandt's deceitfulness. Although they had only known each other for several hours, she needn't condemn Trent of any wrongdoing. A sudden awareness surged to every part of her body. Maybe they were soul mates. Naomi started to enter foreign territory and decided to leave it there.

"Tell me how you'd treat a woman compared to Henry?"

"I'd wine, dine and treat her with respect."

"What about dancing?"

Trent made a deep-throated chuckle. The noise startled Naomi. He quickly changed the subject. "I believe it'll stop raining soon."

"I hope so. Where did you say we are?"

"At the Oasis."

Naomi pushed her back deeper into the old material covered dull red couch. "I asked you earlier is this the Oasis; you told me no. You lied. Henry also informed me this is the Peterson's place."

"Not exactly," said Trent.

Naomi focused on the man. The light from the fire showed off his broad shoulders and deep chest. His damp jeans started to steam. Feeling angry, she unknowingly allowed a grin to slip from the side of her mouth.

"I saw you smile."

"I didn't," sighed Naomi, watching Trent's chest rise.

"I'm the middle son of Mr. Stanton who owns the Oasis and surrounding area. Fifty kilometers north of this place is the actual Oasis. The surrounding area is five hundred square kilometers. The size of the Oasis is forty thousand square acres, or should I say, the Oasis is the shape of a football field."

"An oval!" shrieked Naomi.

Trent nodded.

Naomi scrunched her nose. "There's nothing out here except storms, dust, and Henry. He also mentioned he's your neighbor."

"Yes, he's our closest neighbor. He lives one-hour south of this house. The Oasis is the second most beautiful thing I've ever seen."

"What's the first?" questioned Naomi.

Trent chuckled on his way out of the room.

CHAPTER NINE

NAOMI FINISHED dressing in dry, warm blue jeans and a black button up shirt. She slipped her feet into new white runners and walked into the kitchen.

Trent smiled the moment she entered the room. "Now you look the part of a Jillaroo. The way you look right now could easily melt any man."

"What about the one I'm facing?"

"You sure do. I'll go rustle up some grub."

Naomi's eyebrows angled to a point, wrinkling her brow. "Grub?" she questioned.

"If you want to fit in out here you have to call food, grub."

"You don't strike me as a man who is too familiar with a kitchen?"

"If you're trying to find out if I can cook, I'd rate myself less than average."

"Maybe I should give you some lessons. Sit at the table and watch what I do."

Trent watched Naomi dart around the room, from the stove to the pantry then back to the narrow pantry several times. She looked up at his bewildered face and giggled.

"How did you know what food to bring if you're not good at cooking?"

"I had a shopping list. I had finished stowing everything in the plane when you arrived."

"Who made the shopping list?"

"Gayle," answered Trent.

"Who's Gayle?"

"Do I hear a hint of jealousy in your voice?"

"No, why should there be? We're not an item."

"In that case, I don't have to tell you who Gayle is."

"Another secret," moaned Naomi.

An older man opened the kitchen door and walked into the room like he owned the place. "I can smell food cookin'."

Naomi studied the man. His long silver hair matched his beard. His torn jeans and muddy boots were, she thought, a typical outback look. His blue button up shirt barely covered his massive beer gut.

"Roy Davey, I wondered when you would show your face?" Trent reached out his hand.

"Forget the handshake, I'm not in a good mood. I won't stay long. I have a message for your father."

"This is Naomi," mentioned Trent, palming his hand towards her.

"Nice to meet you, Miss."

"It's good to hear polite words."

"I can tell you're a city gal," he snorted, nodding sharply.

"How?" questioned Naomi.

"You smell like city folk."

"I'm sorry I don't stink like a cow."

"I say what I mean."

"What's the message?" asked Trent, folding his arms.

"The bank has made an offer to buy me place. It's too good to refuse."

"I thought you said you'd never sell."

"I'm not selling. The bank's given me seven days to walk off me land."

As Naomi watched the man from over the stirring of a boiling pot of water, she noticed his face showed no emotion while he informed Trent of the terrible news. 'Steel on the outside, a blubbering mess on the inside,' she thought.

"I'm sorry to hear the news," said Trent.

"If you want to buy me land, think up a good offer. Maybe we'll do a deal. The contest is between you and the bank."

"Six months ago, dad might have jumped at the chance for another 2000 acres; not now."

"Why? I've offered you me land on a silver plate."

"It's the Tax office. They want to take our land too."

Naomi's brow wrinkled when she heard Trent's confession. Her mind steamed harder than the contents of the boiling pot she'd been stirring. She wanted to know more. Up to date the only thing she knew about outback people; they believed land to be the most precious thing in the world. To make them sell seemed un-comprehensible.

"Anyways," continued Davey. "Henry is in the truck. We got to get going. We saw you landing the plane extra fast. We came over to find out if you were okay. I'm pleased you're safe. This storm's a real kicker."

"Thanks for showing you care."

"I'll have it known I didn't want to come over; me Mrs. ordered me."

Trent nodded. Although they sounded like they hated each other neither one seemed willing to be the first to back down so the other could have a niche.

'Both stubborn as each other,' thought Naomi. She wondered if something bad happened would either come running. The minute things returned to normal again she felt convinced they'd revert to disliking each other.

Davey studied Naomi from head to feet. He used his elbow to dig Trent in the ribs. "She's a bit of all right for a city gal. I don't usually give out any advice especially to you or your father. If I, were you, I'd do everything I could to keep her by my side. Look after this one."

"I'll keep your advice under my hat."

"One more thing. I have to tell you Henry bumped the lid off the large box. When I walked past, it was empty."

"It's okay; I'll find Charlie later. He won't have gone too far."

Davey waved goodbye and ran out into the rain.

Naomi thrust the plate of bacon and eggs at Trent. They both sat and ate hungrily. She watched the man watching her. She just couldn't put her finger on the reason why she felt drawn to the man.

"The meal tasted great."

"I'm pleased you liked it." Naomi watched Trent take his empty plate to the sink and start to wash it. 'I'm going to find out the answers to my questions, Trent Stanton, if it's the last thing I do,' she thought inwardly.

Naomi's thoughts tumbled over and over in her mind as she scraped the last morsel of food from her plate. Hunching her shoulders, she said with a sigh. "Three o'clock in the afternoon and the sun looks as though it's about to break through the clouds."

Trent nodded in agreement.

"You didn't look at the sky. Are you going to take my word for it?"

"I don't need to believe you, I can tell."

"How?" quizzed Naomi.

"The wind has dropped."

In a few minutes the sun broke through the clouds. The water in the dam sparkled in the warming rays. Trent finished the dishes then walked across the room to the window. He let a low whistle slip.

Naomi looked down his arm, following his gaze. She looked puzzled.

"What are you staring at?"

"The dam hasn't been this full in years. Care for a swim?"

Naomi answered politely. "No, thanks."

"Come on. A nice swim will do you a world of good." Trent wrapped his arms around Naomi's waist, lifting her into the air. "It's going to be a stinker for the remainder of the day. You city girls need to unwind. The best medicine is swimming, outback style."

Naomi kicked Trent in the shin. "Trent, no!"

"Do you always get your way, city girl?"

She shook her fist at his face. "Not always. I just want to be treated like a lady. Now put me down."

"I understand," said Trent, allowing Naomi's feet to touch the floor.

Naomi placed her arm over the country boy's shoulder. "I'm sorry for snapping. It has nothing to do with you; it's me."

"That's a relief. I thought..." Trent's sentence abruptly ended.

"You thought what?" Naomi quizzed. She leaned towards Tent, hoping not to miss a single letter of a whispered confession.

"It doesn't matter."

Naomi bit her bottom lip, eyeballing the man. It's another secret to add to her ever-increasing questions. Shaking her head, she looked directly at his eyes. "If you walk me to the dam, I'll try my hardest to swim."

"Try? What's there to try about?"

"Not everyone can swim."

Trent focused on Naomi's frightened green eyes. "Are you trying to tell me you can't swim?"

Naomi lowered her gaze, focusing on the wood grain in the floorboards. She wanted to find a crack in a board so she could disappear.

"Yes." Her voice sounded weak at best.

"I'm sorry for embarrassing you. I didn't know."

"I keep it a secret. Kaite, my best friend, is the only one who knows."

"I promise I'll never tell your secret to anyone."

"There's one more thing; I didn't bring a bathing suit."

"Due to the fact you can't swim?" finished Trent. He reached out and dragged her in close.

"Yes." Naomi leaned her head against his chest. She stood listening to the rhythm of his heart. It suddenly quickened.

"Come on; I have the perfect solution."

Trent led Naomi to a black overnight bag, unzipped the top and drove his hand deep inside.

Naomi's giggles broke into laughter when Trent turned the bag upside down. She watched amused as Trent sifted through one pair of blue jeans, three shirts, one white, one black, one wet, muddy shirt and a blue open-neck shirt.

"I'll wear the blue one."

"Are you sure? Why don't you wear a dry one?"

"Trent, the blue button up shirt is the only one long enough to cover. Besides, why wet another shirt?"

"I'll meet you at the dam," he quipped, walking off.

Naomi marched down the hallway to the bathroom. In front of the mirror, she slipped into the wet shirt. The material felt cold and hung heavy from her shoulders. She pushed her feet into her damp runners and set off towards the dam.

'The outback man is right. Inside an hour, the humidity will be stifling,' Naomi surmised. She caught a glimpse of Trent halfway to the dam. Naomi quickly settled into a comfortable running style.

"What on earth are you wearing?" she asked, catching him up.

Trent chuckled. "A black towel."

"Are you wearing anything else?"

"Nothing," he answered seriously.

Naomi swallowed her excitement at the uncertainty of what might transpire over the next hour. Reaching out, she took hold of his hand. With a sideways stare, she watched him walking next to her. Naomi's heart pounded harder. The closer they got to the dam the hotter she felt.

Trent didn't bother to stop, to sum up the cold water. He threw his towel at a fence post and dived in. Naomi stood gob-smacked as her eyes feasted again on his ice cream cone shaped body. He surfaced near the middle of the dam, beckoning her in. Naomi walked to the water's edge. Stepping out of her runners her bare feet sunk into the mud. Trent dived. When he surfaced, he grabbed her ankles. Naomi squealed and flopped down into the mud.

"There's nothing more invigorating than a cold, mud, bath," grumbled Naomi, sarcastically.

"Come on in."

"The mud feels horrible."

Trent marched out of the water. He picked her up in an effortless sweep of an arm and carried her into the water. He patiently taught Naomi the freestyle swimming stroke, with a genuine interested expression as she slowly increased her strokes.

"Naomi, I want to discuss the bet we made back at the airport."

"I'm listening. What's on your mind?"

"I want to call the bet null and void."

"Is this a new way of winning?"

Trent looked directly at her eyes. His easy-going expression faded.

"You win by default. At the first opportunity, I'll give you that dance."

Naomi went to shake his hand. "I'll agree to your demands if you tell me more about yourself."

Trent lifted his arms as if he had finally surrendered. "Okay, what do you want to know?"

"Why do you carry the rope clipped to your belt, and I want to know why your family is about to lose the Oasis?"

"You are an extremely nosy person, Miss Fitzgerald."

"I sure am."

"I'll spill the beans after you kiss me."

Naomi shook her head suspiciously. She needed to keep her mind in check if she wanted to discover what made this country man tick. She couldn't afford to make a mistake.

"You play a good game of poker," taunted Trent.

"I have been known to."

Trent slipped back into waist deep water. "Come in; I won't bite."

"I feel safer back here."

"Okay. I'll have you know you forced me into it. I have a great idea, how about we get dressed so we can talk in a more comfortable place.

You look a little on the cold side." Trent swam to the edge of the dam. He walked up the muddy bank in full view.

Naomi lost her breath, watching the naked man wrap the towel around his narrow waist, marching off towards the house. She instinctively followed.

Trent looked already clean and wore shorts by the time Naomi closed in on the crude, effective outside shower. Two wine barrels were in a tree above head height. A twist of the wooden plug on the bottom of the barrel saw clean water flowing.

Naomi scrunched her nose. "Where's the privacy?"

Trent glared at her. "If you want a shower, this is it."

"I'll use the one inside the house."

Trent grabbed Naomi by the arm to stop her from walking off.

"Let me go," she insisted.

Trent pulled Naomi in close, tightening his grip.

"You're hurting me."

Naomi felt his breath brushing her cheeks. She could tell he wasn't happy at having to tell his story. She shouldn't expect him to say anything about his private life. She felt disappointed at pushing the point. When Trent relaxed his grip Naomi stepped back, glad to have space between them.

"Oh! no you don't city girl. Nothing ever gets away from me," boasted Trent.

"You're a tease."

Trent pulled Naomi in close again. This time, she leaned into the pull. Her action made them fall towards the mud. She heard a squelch. Trent groaned when his back hit the ground. Naomi came down hard on his chest. Both looked lovingly at the other. Trent blushed at seeing Naomi's reddening face. Instead of pushing her off, Trent wrapped his arms around her. She felt imprisoned. Her brain started yelling to slap his smiling face while her heart seemed to be saying something totally different. She tossed into the mix her two opposite ideas.

Her heart won.

Naomi stopped struggling. She brought her hands forward, folding her arms across his chest.

"Is this where I apologize for being huffy and running off?"

"It's a good start," Naomi whispered.

"I'm at your mercy," complained Trent. "You have me a shackled prisoner."

"A big strong man like you, don't make me laugh."

"See I can't move," informed Trent, trying to wriggle his way out from underneath Naomi.

"You could easily throw me off using one arm."

"Yes, I could quite easily accomplish the task," said Trent.

"I dare you to try."

"I don't want to show off."

Snuggling in closer, Naomi chuckled. Trent's skin felt hard from his bulging taut muscles. On a sigh, she closed her eyes. She felt at home, snuggling close to a man who has too many secrets. For the first time in her life, she felt safe in a man's arms. Unexpectedly her vow to Kaite surfaced, making her frown at the thought. Why did she vow such a childish thing? She tried to block out the words by cuddling Trent harder.

"Are you comfortable?"

Naomi nodded and hid her smile by biting her bottom lip.

"Your skin feels cool. Are you cold?" asked Trent.

"No."

"If that's the truth, then you must be thinking something?"

Naomi lifted her head off Trent's chest. "I have been thinking about the secrets you keep locked inside your head."

"I hate torture. I'll confess."

"Start talking big boy." Naomi smiled at his pouting lip.

"I carry the rope on my belt because I'm a rodeo champion."

Naomi arched her back. Her eyes widened at the confession.

"Henry is my opposition. He's never won against me. It's the only reason why his father hates my family. A few years ago, I approached my father, suggesting I should throw the next annual championship. I thought it might help to resolve the issue and they'd be friends again. Dad refused the offer. We agreed if Roy Davey couldn't accept the fact his son might always be second it is bad luck."

Trent let a grin slip.

"What's the look for?"

"Father said the Davey's clan needed to suck it up."

"The annual championships, when are they?"

"It's the bush bash in the nearest town from here. It's fast approaching."

"Shouldn't you be practicing?"

"I don't need to practice. If I find a stray cow or I see a fence post or a city girl, I use my rope."

"You'd rope a city girl?"

"Only the pretty ones," admitted Trent.

"How many pretty ones have you seen?"

"Only one," he whispered.

Naomi portrayed a hurt expression.

"Only you. It's no trouble to say, you're easy on the eyes."

Although Naomi blushed after hearing the compliment, she wanted to probe further. "I feel bad your father, and Henry's father are refusing to talk."

"I can't change the fact."

"I'm on your father's side," stated Naomi.

"I'm sure he'd love to hear that."

"To me it sounds like you have a humble family."

"The good book says we should be."

"Are you religious folk too?"

"Of course," replied Trent. "The only problem in my life is the girl I once liked."

"Your ex-flame?" cut in Naomi. She immediately felt pangs of jealousy over the girl she'd never met.

"Yes. She's Henry's sister. She lives twenty kilometers from the Oasis."

"She's not Gayle?"

"No, Gayle is my brother's wife, though she's a bit of alright. I must add you're one hundred times prettier than her."

Naomi's cheeks instantly turned a bright red color. "Tell me about the Oasis?" she asked.

"The government wants our land. They've always wanted our land ever since they gave it to my family for free. When they discovered how fertile the land was, they wanted it back. My great grandfather refused. He didn't make things easy for us by telling them there's gold in the ground. The land is perfect for cows, nothing else."

"How did he obtain the land for free?"

"We have to get going. Father is expecting us."

Trent pushed Naomi off him and prepared to stand.

Naomi couldn't decide whether she felt disappointed or not, seeing how he didn't answer her question. She respected his decision not to say. Changing tact, she continued.

"Why don't you write to the government telling them firmly, no, you can't have the land?"

"We tried. The government advised us we owe them fifty thousand dollars in back taxes. Pay up or get out."

"Borrow from the bank. When they have what they want, you'll be surprised how quick they'll leave you alone."

"We did try that idea. They informed us we owed them a further three thousand dollars. We again borrowed the money. Twelve months later they said we owed them ten thousand. They won't stop until we're off the land. The government is doing the same to Davey's farm."

"I'm sorry for prying," whispered Naomi.

"It's okay. Unless you know how to find fifty thousand bucks in two weeks, we're off the land, heading to who knows where."

Naomi almost choked at hearing the words. She leaned forward, kissing his forehead. She stood, hovering over the man.

"Come on; I've work to do. On your feet Mr. Trent Stanton," Naomi ordered, in a military voice.

"What's wrong? You've jumped up like our Jack Russell pups."

"Come on. We have to get to the Oasis. I have to talk to your father."

"You can't wait to meet my family?"

"Trent, don't take my news the wrong way. I work for the tax office. I might be able to help."

"My father's a proud man. He won't take any form of help, especially from a woman."

"He's going to have to, whether he wants to or not."

"If you can help, it would be a Godsend. That said, it's time to head for home."

"The first thing I have to do is get clean. I also need to go to the lady's room," called Naomi, walking off towards the house. She looked over her shoulder at Trent. "Where's the toilet?"

"It's around back, near the wood shed. Be careful of the spiders."

Naomi made a flippant hand gesture. Walking around the corner of the house, she glanced at the motorbike. It looked almost a pile of dry mud. She walked behind the small shed and found a wooden structure. It appeared to be two metres tall and no more than one metre square. She opened the door, viewing the room.

"The bush toilet looks worse than the bush shower. Trent calls it an outhouse. I call it a broken-down cabinet. A one metre square box with a bent nail for a doorknob. At least there are four walls and a door." She screwed her nose up at the angle of the door. "I doubt if this place has ever been cleaned."

Naomi entered, studying the wooden seat. "I can't see any spiders."

Feeling something slide across her water-soaked runners, she looked down at the hardened wet dirt. She didn't know whether to scream or cry.

Trent's frantic yell sounded louder than the low throb of the plane's twin engines. The tone in his voice belonged to a person who sounded petrified.

"Naomi, before you enter the outhouse, there's something I forgot to mention, something extremely important."

Trent took a short cut by clambering over the woodpile. He called again more urgent. Naomi could plainly hear the panic in his voice. She started tapping her foot on the ground, waiting for him to arrive.

He sprinted up to the outhouse, rope in hand. Stopping to study the scene, he dropped the rope, looking puzzled at seeing an empty makeshift toilet. Naomi watched him scratch his head while walking around. Eventually, he saw her watching him.

"Excuse me," she said, stepping calmly away from the wood pile.

Trent stood facing the city chic. His eyes were wider than golf balls. His face had drained of color.

"Have you seen a ghost, or are you trembling due to the fact you have lost something about two metres long which slithers, across the ground?" asked Naomi.

Trent's shoulders slumped. His face flushed red. "Yes."

"I believe this might be the living creature you stowed in the large box," stated Naomi, thrusting the python at him.

"I forgot to let you know about Charlie. When you were asleep, I brought him inside the house. I thought you might be scared if I mentioned the snake. Sorry."

"I love snakes, especially Pythons. My flat-mate owns a female."

"Flat-mate?" asked Trent.

"Could it be you're slightly jealous?"

"Maybe a little," he admitted.

"Her name is Kaite."

Trent took possession of the snake, draping it across his shoulders.

"How on earth did Charlie escape the house?"

"Henry bumped the lid off the box. Charlie knows his way around here. He must have found a crack in the floor. I lived in hope I'd find Charlie before you saw him."

Naomi took the snake back and cuddled him. "He's a beautiful specimen. Where did you find him?"

"When my family bought this place six months ago, we discovered him coiled up in the laundry. He never ventured far from the house. By the time my brother and I finished fixing this place Charlie seemed to want to be around us. I couldn't leave him, so I decided to adopt the snake. I named him Charlie."

"Trent, do you have any more secrets?"

"A few," he whispered. Grinning, he picked up the length of rope, clipping it back on to his belt.

"I'm impressed at the way you can wind a rope."

"I'm not a rodeo champ by accident."

Naomi snarled inwardly. 'Trent, starting now, I'm going to derive a plan to make you confess every one of your secrets.'

"How handy are you at using the rope?"

"Care for a demonstration?"

"Sure."

Pointing to a fence-post, Trent unbuckled the rope. In a slick move, he swung the loop in circles several times above his head. At the precise moment, he let the noose go then closed his eyes. The large noose flew through the air, landing over the fence post.

"Not bad for a stationary object," Naomi taunted.

Trent re-wound the rope, clipping it to his belt. "Don't move."

Naomi watched him march in the direction of the house. Jumping on the motorbike, he easily kicked started it. At speed, he came roaring back. Trent completed a few doughnuts in the dirt. He displayed a proud expression, standing on the seat while the bike roared towards the fence post. One foot worked the throttle of the bike the other foot looked firmly planted into the seat. He winked at Naomi. Unclipping the rope, he started rotating the noose above his head. In seconds, he sent the rope sailing through the air. The noose landed in the exact center of the fence post. Trent jumped off the bike, landing feet first in the mud.

"I'm impressed. You should enter your tricks into the rodeos," cheered Naomi.

"I don't have to; they expect me to turn up. We have had enough fun, it's time to go."

CHAPTER TEN

THE PLANE ascended steadily in the dying wind, leveling off at one hundred and thirty-seven feet. The storm had been swept away. Ahead of the plane was a pale blue sky all the way to the horizon.

"Soon you'll see the full view of the Oasis," said Trent.

"I'm looking forward to seeing it."

A shiver shot through Naomi's body from her head to her feet. Could the feeling mean she'd already started to fall in love? She felt tempted to lean sideways and kiss Trent and wrap her arms around him. Inwardly, she yelled a stern warning. Find out what made him tick. Don't fall in love with someone who seemed to have a lot of secrets.

The plane changed direction, banking slightly. Naomi gripped her seat to stop from leaning against Trent. She sighed in relief when the plane was again flying level.

"You do realize having too many secrets is bad for you? It could be the reason why you're still single," blurted Naomi.

"Maybe," answered Trent.

To Naomi finding out the answers to her questions seemed harder than digging a deep hole in hardened clay using a kid's plastic hand shovel. Noting the concentration etched on Trent's face, Naomi focused on the desert landscape. She spied a pack of kangaroos basking in the sun and a herd of cows eating near a small dam. She counted twenty-seven before they slipped from view.

The next scene to catch her attention was the slow turning windmills dotting the landscape. They snaked in an endless line to the horizon. Each one appeared to be anchored to the side of a dam a kilometer apart.

Naomi thought. 'I wonder if there's an underground river feeding the dams.' She cupped a hand above her eyes to form a shield so she could follow the line of dams to the edge of her vision, then back to the Peterson's house. She felt satisfied at discovering the desert's secret.

Glancing at Trent, she wondered if he knew about the underground river.

"Can I ask you something?"

"I'll answer your question to the best of my ability." Trent looked at the plane's instruments then switched his attention to Naomi. "You sure are the most beautiful sight out here," he whispered.

Naomi felt unprepared for the statement. To prevent her cheeks from reddening, she pretended not to hear what he said.

"How did you get an education?"

"Your question is easy to answer. Education came through the school of the air. I came top of my class."

"My teacher spoke about the system when I was in sixth grade. I'm not totally convinced learning over the radio is a good thing."

"It mightn't be. Out in the middle of Australia, there's no other way of learning."

"What about school friends?"

"Friends were few. The voices of the other kids were great. We sent photos of ourselves to each other so we could have a visual idea who the voice belonged to."

"I believe it would be difficult to fall in love out here in the middle of nowhere." Naomi watched Trent from the corner of her eye waiting to see his reaction.

Trent looked out his side of the window. "Three months after turning sixteen I thought I had fallen in love. At that time, the girl lived one-hundred and three kilometers from the Oasis."

Naomi looked out the plane's window, raising an eyebrow.

"I snuck out of our house one Friday night after dinner. I rode a motorbike to her house in the dark. I woke her as the rooster crowed."

"Did you get into a lot of trouble?"

"Some. Mary-Lou's father didn't take too kindly to my presence. He was shocked when he found out I'd ridden across the outback on a dirt bike in the dark. He let me stay the entire day. Sun up the next day he fueled my bike and sent me on my way."

"What did your father say?"

"My father suggested I don't do it again."

"What about the girl?"

"After I left for home, she never talked to me again."

"That is a shame."

"No, it's a good thing. If anything, else happened, I might never have met you."

Naomi didn't know where to look. She felt happy he quoted such a nice statement. It had been a long time since someone said anything positive about her.

Trent reached for Naomi's hand. Raising it to his lips, he kissed her knuckles. The move sent a shiver into the middle of Naomi's back. Instead of dispersing, the feeling lingered.

"If I must compare you to the beauty of the Oasis, you'd win every time. The Oasis is the second most beautiful thing out here. There is no comparison between you and the Oasis."

Naomi certainly didn't expect such a solid statement. When she spoke, her voice sounded weak. "Are there any more secrets you'd like to share?"

Trent remained silent. He guided the plane downwards, leveling off at seventy-nine feet. Naomi spied an old deserted house. In spots the fencing was missing, blown down by other storms. A large metal gate looked half buried in the mud.

"Naomi, if you look ahead the Oasis is about to come into view," said Trent.

"It's been a few minutes. You want to talk now?" She looked sideways willing him to open his mouth to tell everything.

"I only talk when I have something important, I want to say."

"You told me the same thing a while ago."

"Yes, I know I did."

Naomi returned her gaze to the desert below. "It's fantastic," she whispered. "The area does take your breath away. It's unbelievable. How is it all possible?" Slowly she returned her gaze back to Trent's smiling face. She wanted to test the man of his honesty and finally discovered a way. "You never did explain the details on how your father found the place?"

"I have already mentioned my father didn't discover the Oasis. My great grandfather stumbled across it by accident."

Naomi felt impressed at Trent's honesty and seemingly endless patience. She sat next to him wondering what it might take for him to lose his cool?

"How the Oasis was formed, no one knows. I've also asked the school of the air. No one has an answer to my question. Some say a large meteorite hit the Earth millions of years ago, which left the oval shaped crater. Others have said a river formed the Oasis. Every time it rains the river leading into the Oasis cascades over the side. The water falls one hundred feet to the river below. The main entry point is the waterfall. Don't ever be in the river when she's flowing. Even though the water's not deep, I rescue several cows every year from the river."

"Using your trusty rope?" cut in Naomi.

Trent nodded

"No wonder you carry it on your belt."

The plane circled the edge of the giant oval in the ground. Flying over the fringe, the plane dived, following the waterfall and skimmed the tree tops.

"You can see why we always have plenty of water and green grass. Now you understand why the area is perfect for cows."

Naomi studied the entire fertile land. The grass looked a rich dark green. An abundance of cows freely roamed. She estimated there might be at least a thousand head. Focusing on the river, her gaze traced it to the other end of the land where the water disappeared underground.

The plane roared from one end of the river to the other, banked then headed up river again.

"You have four houses close together," mentioned Naomi.

"Mine is the newest looking one. I moved in three weeks ago. Everyone has to build their own. It is father's rules. My parents and my older sister live in the two-storey mansion. Next house in line is my eldest brother's and his wife. My house is tacked on the end."

"The Oasis is a beautiful place," remarked Naomi. "I can see why you don't want to leave. I still can't understand how you can compare its beauty to me. The Oasis is in a field of its own."

Trent locked his gaze on Naomi. She felt an arc of electricity shoot between them. They smiled at each other simultaneously. A new question flashed into Naomi's mind. Did he build the house for her?

Trent turned his head away and looked out of the plane's windscreen.

Naomi copied his move, disappointed the moment had ended so abruptly.

CHAPTER ELEVEN

TRENT PREPARED to land the plane by lining up a dirt path which ran along the entire length of the fast-flowing river. The usual whine of the plane's engines slowed. The ground came up quickly.

"Where does the water go?" asked Naomi, watching the river flow towards the cliff face.

"It pours into an underground tunnel. In the dry season about four years ago, I dived into the cave and followed the waist deep water for half an hour. It seemed endless. Through research, I found a map. It showed me the river ended at the sea near Darwin."

The plane landed gracefully and stopped next to the river. Trent cut the engines and opened the door. The north wind felt strong. The sun felt warm against Naomi's skin.

"Every dam between here and the house we landed at earlier has tapped into the underground river," quoted Naomi.

"You catch on quick," said Trent.

"You haven't explained in detail how your family came across this place."

"Didn't I?"

"No. You avoided details of my question by changing the plane's course one degree."

"You're a very observant young lady."

"I'm curious."

"Also, intelligent. I love a woman who is intelligent."

'One for me,' Naomi thought.

"Discovering the Oasis had been a massive coincidence. My great grandfather's best mate Tom conned him into selling everything he owned back in England. Free land in Australia he said. They came out together dragging their family with them. When they reached Australia, they were laughed out of the small wooden governor's shack. Unperturbed by the set-back, my great grandfather conned the government of the time into giving him anything he discovered right here. The remainder speaks for itself."

"Fantastic family history!" exclaimed Naomi.

"I've confessed too much. Don't forget, you're supposed to be here for work." Trent unbuckled his seat belt and stepped down from the plane. "Whatever you do, stay away from the river. She's moving the fastest I've ever seen after the recent storm."

Naomi focused on a group of riders who were approaching the plane at speed. She guessed they came from the main house. Each member of the group rode a magnificent looking horse. The group resembled characters straight out of a western movie. She undid her seat belt and stepped down from the plane.

"The posse has arrived," she said, pointing.

Trent flashed her a thunderstorm expression.

"I'm only kidding."

Naomi watched each rider pull back on the reins of their horse and step onto the ground. The boots of each rider sank slightly in the softened mud.

"Welcome home," chorused the riders in unison.

Naomi paid special attention to a tall man wearing a cowboy hat, blue jeans, and a plain pale blue button up shirt. The man's stomach looked relatively flat for his age. He took off his large hat and outstretched his hand. His thick grey head of hair looked tidy. His broad shoulders were square; his posture, straight. He stood military style.

Trent shook the man's hand then palmed his free hand towards his companion.

"Father, this is the single package I informed you about, Miss Naomi Fitzgerald; Mr. Earl Stanton."

"We meet at last. Sir, it's urgent we talk."

Stanton squared himself to Naomi, revealing a picture of the Oasis tattooed on his forearm.

"I have some reservations about hiring a young lady from the city. I did expect at least one bloke."

"Father, I did explain Naomi is the only person."

"Earl, help the young lady to feel welcome."

Naomi searched for the friendly voice. It came from the mouth of a tall, thin, middle-aged woman who held the reins of a brown mare.

"I'm Mrs. Margaret Stanton," she announced, stepping forward. "My husband only looks mean. When you get to know him, you'll find he's nothing more than a giant teddy bear."

Earl Stanton's chuckle quickly changed into a full belly laugh. "Glad you could come. I need all the help I can get."

The remainder of the group rushed to Naomi's side. Trent introduced each one of his family members in turn.

"Pleased to meet you," said a man stepping forward. His grin widened; his blue eyes seemed to flash.

'You have to be Trent's older brother,' Naomi thought. 'Your build is similar, and you wear the same style clothing as your father.'

"Enough greetings," bellowed Stanton. "We've work to do. Son, we'll see you at the house for dinner."

Trent nodded as the group made a move to mount their horse.

"Mr. Stanton, I must talk to you," called Naomi, watching the group start to ride off.

Disappointed at being ignored, Naomi faced the one remaining rider.

"I'm Mitch, Trent's younger brother. I'll be twenty-five next week."

"Pleased to meet you," said Naomi.

Mitch let the reins of his horse drop so he could reach out his hand. He grabbed Naomi's wrist. He lowered his head and kissed her knuckles.

"Hey," yelled Trent.

"I can tell he's been hanging around you," laughed Naomi. She felt deeply touched by the fuss. Trent's sudden outburst tickled her to the core.

Charlie lifted the lid of the box and slithered out of the plane. He made his way towards the last remaining horse, curling around its foreleg. The horse jerked his head when it felt the snake. Charlie lifted his head. The horse reared up, accidently bumping Naomi towards the river. She rolled her ankle in the soft mud and landed on her back in waist deep water. She shivered from the sudden cold. Almost instantly she felt the water start to suck her down. Trying desperately to stand in the fast-moving current, Naomi knew the river already held her firmly in its grip. If she didn't stand immediately, the river would sweep her off towards the cave mouth. Using every ounce of strength, she could gather, Naomi only managed to push her hands into the air. To stay calm, she tried to remember the swimming style Trent taught her. She attempted a few feeble strokes.

Trent whirled around when he heard the splash. Naomi surfaced, gasping for air. She locked her gaze on Trent's horror-stricken face. Before she could yell a word, the water swirled around her, pulling her down for the second time.

'I feel incredibly calm,' Naomi thought. 'Maybe this is what people went through when they were about to die.'

The washing machine style river made her tumble head over heels. Naomi locked her elbows. The act successfully stopped her tumbles. Her feet scraped the hard ground. She winced in pain as her ankle rolled again. Naomi's head broke the surface. She didn't waste a second, quickly gulping a life-saving breath before the water again swallowed her whole.

'Trent, where are you. I need you to use the rope,' Naomi screamed inwardly. 'I must be dreaming. I fell asleep lying on my bed. Yes, this is a dream. In a few seconds, I'll wake to find myself wrapped up in the bed linen.'

Naomi's head broke the surface again. She managed to take another deep breath. A short, sharp scream followed. Looking upstream she saw Trent running.

"This is no dream," she mumbled. Lifting her arm towards her hero, she yelled. "Trent, save me. Use your rope."

"I'm coming. Hold your arm up," Trent yelled.

Naomi did what he said. She watched him unclip the rope from his belt and start the rope circling above his head. The gap between them quickly grew wider. She saw him gather the rope and clip it back on to his belt.

'What's his idea? So much for my cowboy hero,' Naomi screamed inwardly. She switched her thoughts from Trent to Kaite. She felt sad she didn't get the chance to make a phone call to her to find out what she might be doing. Naomi felt proud at knowing the fact she'd probably be getting ready to go out and have a good time at a nightclub.

Returning her thoughts back to her dilemma, Naomi could feel her body beginning to go numb from the cold. Her lungs started to ache. She tried to think how long she could hold her breath. The only time she ever tried she failed to get past ten seconds. At realizing she might have been holding her breath for eight seconds, Naomi began to panic. Surely, she could hold her breath for at least fifteen seconds. Naomi exhaled a small amount of air hoping the act might help to stop the ache in her lungs.

It didn't.

Naomi's left shoulder dug into the hard ground. Excruciating pain shot throughout her body. Life as she knew it began to slip away.

Naomi barely felt the tug. She opened her eyes, looking down at her right leg. She felt disappointed her new jeans were finished, ripped open from the knee down to her ankle and her hip had scraped against a rock, ripping her pocket away, exposing her thigh. Her eyes widened when she felt the edge of the whirlpool.

'The cave entrance must be close,' she reasoned.

Naomi commenced rotating her arms in a desperate freestyle swim. Ascending to the surface proved to be difficult. She wanted to kick herself for not heeding her mother's warning about learning to swim. She closed her eyes thinking the end must only be seconds away. Trent's face flashed into her mind. Why didn't he bother to rescue her? Did he lie about everything? The spark she felt for him must have been fake. She made up her mind he must be just the pilot. He'd successfully strung her along just like the other men who had entered her life over the years. She felt sad no one ever discovered the perfect gift. After her death, she imagined Trent standing in the middle of the local pub laughing, having a joke at her expense. Kaite did warn her to stay in the city. Now she could kick herself for not listening.

Naomi pushed Trent's reoccurring face from her mind. Her parents and Kaite's image were the ones she wanted to remember at the time of her death. Feeling something hard around her waist, she lifted her hand to attempt to remove it. Everything around her started to go black. Her head broke the surface. She opened her eyes. Her lungs heaved life-saving oxygen. The object of concern felt firmly wrapped around her waist. Looking down she saw tanned skin. Naomi coughed out water and managed to look up.

"G'day. I thought I'd join you for a swim. If you'd given me more notice, I'd have taken off my boots."

"Trent!" Naomi could hardly believe it. If she had died, why was he in her thoughts? "What are you doing?"

"Don't you want to be rescued?"

"Does this mean I'm not dead?"

"Not even close. Have you forgotten what I told you earlier? Nothing gets away from me."

Oxygen flowed quickly through Naomi's body. Her faculties surged. She raised her arms, hugging Trent's neck.

"Whatever happens don't let go. This whirlpool ends up inside the underground tunnel I told you about."

"How are you going to save us both? I can feel the water starting to suck us down."

Trent grinned. "Plan B."

Naomi displayed a pacified look, deciding to let the man do his stuff.

Trent unclipped his rope and tied one end around both of them as they were dragged to the bottom. When his feet touched the ground, he crouched. In one massive show of strength, he pushed off, propelling them both upwards.

They broke surface.

Naomi slipped from his shoulders. She managed to grab Trent's belt buckle with white knuckles. Trent sent the rope sailing through the air, snagging a steel hook 25mm in diameter which someone thoughtfully rammed into the side of the vertical wall of the Oasis. The rope tightened. The pair hung suspended up to their waist in white surging water which threatened to suck them down to the bottom of the vortex and sweep them to their death.

Naomi looked down at the whirlpool. She saw hard ground at the center of the vortex. She gripped Trent's brass belt buckle using every ounce of strength she could muster. She shuddered at the thought of being sucked down into the cave, her lifeless body bouncing underwater for hours, maybe even weeks until it could be found at the beach. Naomi looked up at Trent's azure-colored eyes. She noted their sparkle made him look jovial.

"Why are you so happy?" she asked.

"I saved your life."

Naomi frowned, trying to climb. "I hate to be a party crasher. I have some sad news. The water seems to be rising."

"No, it's not, you are slipping. Hold on."

Naomi watched Trent monkey climb, up the rope, bringing her up out of the water.

"Now it's your turn to help," groaned Trent. "I need you to reach out for the hooked steel rod above your head. When you have a firm grip, you have to let me go."

"I can't. I'm too weak from the cold."

"Yes, you can. The cavalry is almost here."

Naomi looked upstream. She spied the small group of riders galloping up to the mouth of the cave. Mr. Stanton led the charge. Naomi grabbed the steel hook. With a white-knuckle grip, she wrapped her fingers around the cold metal. In a brave attempt, she tried to lift her body free of the water.

"There's no need to climb. Help is at hand," announced Trent.

A lassoed rope fell over Naomi's head. Hanging by one hand, she managed to push her torso through the rope. It quickly tightened. In seconds someone pulled her free of the water.

"Mr. Stanton, you have to save Trent," Naomi urged, collapsing into his arms.

"He can look after himself," he answered.

Stanton placed Naomi gently on the ground next to the river. She opened her mouth to yell at him. Her scream didn't leave her throat. Two hands grabbed her around the waist, heaving her to a standing position.

"Are you okay?"

"Yes, I'll be fine. Thank you for rescuing me. How did you escape the water?"

"I swung myself free."

Mr. Stanton let out a loud belly laugh. The noise sent the group into chuckles.

Naomi's blue face changed to anger red. "Stop laughing at me," she ordered.

Mr. Stanton raised his hand into the air. The group instantly stopped laughing.

"Are you positive, you're okay?" Stanton asked.

Naomi made a slow hesitant nod.

"To set the record straight none of us will ever laugh at you. On behalf of my family, we are overjoyed you are safe."

"Here, here," chorused the group.

"I apologize for flying off the handle. I'm just a little embarrassed."

"Don't be. The accident wasn't your fault. Come on back to the house, we'll have a coffee and scones," instructed an elderly lady from the rear of the pack. "I'll find you a soft towel. Some dry clothes too."

"The lovely lady is my grandmother. She always has freshly baked scones ready to eat," explained Trent.

Naomi studied each person in the small group. "Thanks to everyone for coming to my rescue." When she focused on Stanton's face, she could tell he wasn't at all pleased.

"Girlie, what kind of foolish stunt did you think you were trying to pull? Trent talked me into giving you the job. I think he and I are going to have words later. I need a Jackaroo for two weeks, not a two-bit girl from the city masquerading as a bloke."

Margaret stepped up, placing a hand on her husband's shoulder. She said in a whisper. "Earl, give the young lady a chance."

"No. I'll go so far as to say I'm happy she's okay."

Naomi put her hands on her hips, glaring at Stanton. Trent shook his head, waving her away from the group. Naomi walked off, focusing on Stanton. She surmised he looked to be a man of good character, not how he appeared; tough on the outside. She watched him point towards her a few times before slapping Trent on the shoulder. Naomi didn't know what to make of the whole scene.

When Trent beckoned Naomi over, she quickly walked towards the group. Standing next to Trent, studying his stone-faced expression, her smile could easily melt an ice cube on a cold day.

Mr. Stanton put his hands on his hips, clearing his throat. "Listen, girlie; I'm looking for a Jackaroo, not some two-bit city girl trying to look like a bloke. This, I've already mentioned. Trent should not have talked me into allowing him to bring you here. I'm not sure what you've got in mind. I know you'd never pass for a bloke, you're too shapely."

Naomi folded her arms. "The first thing I want to say to you Mr. Stanton is; don't ever call me girlie again."

"What if I do?"

"I punched the lights out of the last bloke who said it."

Stanton cleared his throat again by coughing into his hand.

"Secondly; I thought being a Jillaroo might be what I needed."

"Is there a third?"

"Yes. I'm not a two-bit girl from the city wanting to look like a bloke."

"Trent told me how you handled Charlie the first time you met him. Any young lady who isn't afraid to handle a two-metre python snake and has the nerve to stand up to me gets my vote. Welcome to the Oasis." Stanton shook Naomi's hand to seal his comment.

"Does this mean I have the job?"

"You do, yes," said Margaret Stanton. "The first thing the job requires you to do is to change into dry clothes. The second part is for you to eat a hot meal."

Naomi faced Trent. "Am I cooking, or are you?"

"I'll do the cooking. Come on; Grandma already has a head start," said Margaret Stanton. She squatted and gathered up Charlie.

Naomi saw the old woman riding off towards the house. "By the look of things, I think we should hurry. She already has a one-hundred metre head start."

CHAPTER TWELVE

TRENT GAVE Naomi the five-cent tour of the large mansion, ending at the upstairs' guestroom. Before walking to the door, he showed her the location of the soft towel cupboard and the bathroom.

"Do you want me to wash your back?" he asked.

"I can manage."

Trent backed out of the room, closing the solid wooden door behind him.

Naomi soaked her mind in the grandeur of the small, exquisite room. Its marble floor, gold tap fittings and the miniature chandelier hanging from the high ceiling looked beautiful.

"Everything in its rightful place," she half whispered, stepping out of her wet clothes. She piled them in a corner and stood under the gold-plated shower rose. She stared at the torrent of water falling on her face. 'Amazing,' she thought. 'Who'd ever dream of a place like this?'

The feeling of the piping hot water rejuvenated Naomi's strength. The hours since meeting Trent started to replay over in her mind. She crumbled to the floor of the shower, sobbing quietly.

"This hot shower beats the cold fast flowing river," she mumbled when her crying finally subsided. "I believe I'm one lucky girl. I could've ended up thousands of miles from the Oasis."

Totally hypnotized by the warm shower water hitting in the exact center of her head, Naomi failed to hear the knock or the bathroom door opening.

"Hello, city girl. Can you hear me?" called Trent.

From the doorway, he could barely see through the fog created by the hot water billowing up from behind the opaque plastic shower curtain. He reached through the gap in the curtain, turning off both taps.

Naomi squealed.

Trent retreated to the door and called again.

"I'm not finished yet."

"You've been in the shower so long I thought you drowned."

Naomi pushed her head into her hands. "Go away," she sobbed.

Trent threw a towel over the shower rail. "Please, get dressed, dinner is ready."

"Give me one minute."

"I'll be waiting to escort you to the table," advised Trent. "Are you okay?"

"I'm fine."

"Why were you sobbing?"

Naomi felt too distraught to know where to begin.

"Explain it after dinner." Trent back stepped out of the small room and closed the door in his wake.

After hearing the bathroom door click shut, Naomi whispered. "You are indeed a gentleman, Trent Stanton."

Naomi rummaged through the pile of dry clothes he had dropped on to the vanity. She was still brushing her hair when she heard a knock.

"Miss Fitzgerald, two minutes has elapsed, it's time for dinner."

"I'm ready."

Naomi slipped her feet into long black boots. Faded blue jeans covered her legs, and a green button up shirt hung from her shoulders. She roughly tied her hair into a ponytail. When she opened the door, she saw Trent nod. She watched him bounding down the stairs. He stood on the first step leaning against the balustrade looking up; a casual expression plastered on his face. He smiled at Naomi when she started down. Trent held out his arm ready to escort her to the dining room table.

The Stanton family watched Trent pull the chair back and wait patiently for Naomi to sit on the wooden red-gum seat.

"Sorry about the clothes. They are the only things I could find at short notice. I want to add; you look perfect," whispered Trent.

Naomi's cheeks took on the look of a dull crimson color. Inwardly she felt totally embarrassed at all the fuss.

Mr. Stanton's wife walked into the room carrying a long pink dressing gown. "Here you are, wear this over your baggy clothes. My son is considerate. He has no idea about women's fashion. Your wet clothes are in the machine. The minute they are washed, I will place them in the drier. They should be ready to wear in about three hours."

"Thank you."

After Mr. Stanton said a short thankful prayer, everyone dug into the perfectly cooked dinner with all the trimmings. The table reminded Naomi of a Christmas dinner. The only thing missing was the printed Christmas napkins and the presents under the tree.

Throughout dinner, Mr. Stanton kept an eye on Naomi and hardly spoke a word at the table.

After finishing her meal, Margaret Stanton threw her napkin on the table, glaring at her husband.

"This silence has to stop," she spat. "Earl, you have to let the Oasis go. Stop trying to keep her. It's beyond saving. You know there's nothing you can do. Those cows have to be gone."

Earl eyeballed his wife. "If you'll excuse me, I'll be in the study." He stood and marched out of the room.

Margaret Stanton clenched her fingers and punched the air. "One of these days I'll give Earl a jab in the nose."

Naomi swallowed her last mouthful of food, looking directly at Mrs. Stanton. "I need to talk to your husband in private. I believe I might be able to help."

"Forget your idea. It's too late." Trent walked to the front door and stepped outside onto the verandah.

Naomi's shoulders drooped in despair. She decided on a different tact by directing her questions at Earl Stanton's wife. Surely, she could make some headway by having her on the same side.

"Why are you getting rid of so many cows? If it's about leaving the land, there must be a way to stay."

Mrs. Stanton started to sob. "There isn't. Trent's correct, it's too late."

"It's never too late. I always try to look on the positive side of things. I believe there's a solution to any problem. It is urgent I speak to Mr. Stanton."

"There is no good solution," croaked Margaret Stanton.

"There has to be."

"After I explain what happened in detail, you'll understand why it's too late."

Naomi listened to the full story, memorizing every word. When Margaret finished the tale, Naomi walked across the floor. Stepping onto the verandah, she looked for Trent. She found him leaning on the railing at the darkest part of the house. Naomi walked slowly up behind him. The smell of tobacco filled the stagnant air.

"It's such a beautiful clear night. The stars look magnificent. You couldn't count them if you tried," Naomi whispered from over his right shoulder. "The crescent moon reminds me of a giant banana hanging low in the sky."

"Yes, it does."

"Your mum told me everything. I'm so sorry."

Trent studied the sky, ignoring the statement. "The stars are nice tonight," he whispered.

"You're making small talk."

"I know."

"The Oasis is a beautiful place."

"After the two weeks are up, I suppose you will be back in the city."

"Yes, at my desk complaining at the lack of help from the office tribe." Naomi let go of a nervous chuckle. "I suppose Brandt and his fox like features will be sniffing around."

"Foxes are sly animals. They sneak around in the dark hoping to find an easy victim," stated Trent.

"He's sly alright. The man fooled, pegged and branded me in one foul swoop."

Trent faced Naomi. "No one should take advantage of a deer."

"What are you talking about?"

Trent answered her question by patting an escaping curl. Naomi felt her knees give way. She groped for the handrail the moment a shiver ran down her back. To disguise her feelings, she closed her eyes and tilted her head upwards towards her hero. Trent lowered his. Naomi wanted the scene to last forever. She wanted to kiss the lips of this handsome outback man like she never kissed a bloke before. She wanted him to take her in his arms. She wanted him to whisk her away to fantasyland. She wanted to live at the Oasis. She wanted an uncomplicated life.

Naomi's thoughts started to mingle into one massive ball. She looked directly at Trent. His warm breath swept her cheeks. He smelt fantastic. His aftershave easily made her fall into a trance.

A muffled noise near the other end of the verandah made Trent look up.

Naomi looked away.

The romantic moment quickly evaporated into the air.

Trent and Naomi spotted a long furry tail belonging to a fox. The animal glanced at the house, its eyes shining in the lights of the verandah.

"It's heading for the chicken pen," announced Trent.

"I suppose you have to go."

"Why?"

"To protect the chickens," sighed Naomi.

"Nothing can get to the chickens. The chook pen has a two-metre-deep wall of metal sheeting buried around the perimeter. The chickens will be fine. Besides, the young chick right here is more precious. She needs looking after. She's new to the Oasis. Four-day old chicks are gorgeous. They can't compare to you, Naomi Fitzgerald."

Naomi's eyes glistened. Tears formed in her eyes. Her cheeks flushed bright red. Trent lovingly wrapped her in his arms.

Again, they both leaned forward at the same time. Naomi's and Trent's lips were almost touching. She knew in her spirit something wonderful had already started. This man who lives in the middle of nowhere seemed wonderful. She felt the pangs of love pull at her heart again. The only thing she needed to do was to allow them to invade her world. If she did, how could it work? Trent is a man who is different from anyone she had ever known. He's the silent type who kept everything inside. She is a city girl, an office worker. Mr. Stanton certainly wouldn't approve. Naomi decided their love could never be.

Naomi broke free of Trent's masculine arms.

"What happened?"

He sounded hurt. What had she done? She tried to make sense of her decision. Maybe her destiny lay somewhere else, the city perhaps or maybe she had grown stubborn over the years.

Naomi walked away, covering her face with her hands. "I'm sorry." She marched to the opposite end of the verandah. Leaning against the railing, she watched Trent looking into the darkness. She saw him looking at her. Then he started walking towards her.

Naomi switched her focus to her feet. She wanted to escape the confrontation. How could she ever manage to explain her innermost thoughts?

Trent's footsteps kept coming. Naomi's heart wanted them to. Her thoughts yelled the opposite. She turned away and looked out over the landscape.

Trent stepped up behind her, putting his hands on her shoulders. She let him massage her neck then allowed him to wrap his arms around her waist. She wanted so much to be a part of his life. She wanted to be a country girl, living at the Oasis. How could Trent believe this could be any more than a two-week fling? After all, they lived in separate worlds. Maybe the Oasis wasn't meant to be. Deep down Naomi felt it might be time to move on. Perhaps one day she'd write every one of her thoughts on paper. In her twilight years, she could read about Trent and the Oasis and what might have been.

"What have you been thinking about?" whispered Trent.

"The cows," answered Naomi, trying not to sound too corny.

"I can't see anything from here."

Trent pulled at Naomi's hair tie, allowing her hair to fall. With his hand, he gently moved a handful away from her neck.

Naomi closed her eyes and waited patiently to discover what he might do next.

The man nibbled at her ear then her neck.

'Forget the washing machine full of thoughts,' she decided inwardly. 'If the Oasis went down, she wanted every moment to count.' Naomi turned around. Facing the cowboy, she thrust her head upwards.

Naomi heard the front door open. Someone stepped onto the verandah. Both looked up. They saw a match ignite. The smell of tobacco filled the air.

"Nice night," called the voice.

"Dad!" called Trent, sounding shocked at being discovered.

Naomi backed away, her eyes widening in horror.

"If you have a few minutes for the job interview, Miss Fitzgerald, I think we should conduct it now."

Naomi straightened her long thick dressing gown. "I'm not dressed for an interview." Flicking her hair behind her ears, she displayed a doubtful look.

Mr. Stanton waved a stubby hand in the air. "It's an informal interview." He stooped, pulling his boots from off his feet. He dropped them noisily on the verandah.

Trent laughed. Mr. Stanton chuckled. Naomi giggled.

Stanton walked over. "I'm not that bad. Call me Earl. I have to confess I do need an extra pair of hands."

"Your wife told me the entire story," cut in Naomi, watching for his angry expression.

It never eventuated.

Earl grunted, exhaling a cloud of smoke into the night sky.

"How good are you at riding a motorbike or a horse?"

"I have to be honest, I'm not an expert at either. I'm a fast learner."

"It's a good start. It'll be Trent's job to teach you. There might come a time when you need at least some experience at both. In 48 hours, the first of many trucks will arrive. In four days, the entire herd of cattle will be gone. In two weeks, we'll fly out of here for the last time."

"Maybe there is a way I could help you save this piece of paradise."

"No, there is no other way. The government wants my land. The land they'll get."

"It doesn't seem fair."

"Lass, life isn't fair. My grandfather would turn in his grave if he knew the reason why we're leaving this place. The government introduced a land tax five years ago, to get me off the land. I am a stubborn man. I'm happy I gave them a run for their money."

"Why does the government think this particular piece of land is so important?"

"They think there's oil or gold under our feet."

Naomi's face turned anger red. "The government can't force you to leave."

"They can. Unless I give them fifty thousand dollars in the next forty-eight hours, the sheriff will be here to evict us."

"Do you love this place?" asked Naomi.

"I'd expect that sort of question from a city girl."

Naomi rolled her eyes, repeating the question.

"Love it," chorused the two men.

"Have you made every tax deduction you can?"

"I don't accept charity," growled Earl.

"It's not charity. It's the law," Naomi exploded.

"I don't claim deductions. Don't seem right."

"For how many years?" Naomi probed.

"My entire life," advised Earl.

Naomi brightened. "You've entered my world. I'm a tax accountant. Lead me to your account books. Let me see what the weather brings."

"No way, my office is off limits to everyone except my family."

Naomi stamped her foot on the verandah. "You're a stubborn man alright Earl Stanton."

He glared, pointing his finger at her. "No one talks to me that way, not even a city girl trying to pass as a bloke for a two-week holiday."

"I'm trying to help you save this place."

"I don't need city folk help. They got me into this mess in the first place. I don't trust your kind. No one sticks their nose into my books." Turning sharply, he marched back inside the house.

"The way I see it you have no choice. You either let me help, or you'll lose this lovely place," called Naomi. By the time, she'd finished talking Earl Stanton had slammed the door shut.

"How sure are you I have the job?" asked Naomi, looking at Trent.

"Positive." He took her by the hand. "Come, I want to show you something."

"I don't have time. I must convince your father I can help."

Trent nodded at his mother who witnessed the entire scene from the lounge room window. As Trent led Naomi by the hand down the verandah steps, Margaret Stanton closed the window curtains.

"Trent, what about the cows, won't we bump into any?"

"No. Years ago, the entire family pitched in to make a cattle grid which encircles the house. It's a moat that doesn't need water. The cattle can't get a firm footing so they can't jump it. The grid is made up of fifty-millimeter-wide metal rollers. Each roller was placed parallel over a ditch about a metre wide."

"What a perfectly natural way to stop cows from straying where you don't want them."

"Exactly. For a city girl, you do catch on quick," said Trent.

"Where are you taking me? You whisked me away from the house so fast I have yet to stake my case on how I can help save the Oasis."

"You'll get your chance. Before the night turns old, there's a place I want to show you. It's a place where we won't be disturbed by anyone."

The pair walked through the dark. Naomi watched a large wooden two storey shed come into view. In the dull moonlight, its structure looked to be well maintained. Trent easily slid the door open, escorting his guest to the stairs. He carried her effortlessly to the top, lifting the small trap door in the floor and carried her to the window. Trent grabbed a set of keys hanging from a nail. He unlatched the long wooden shutters.

"This is a view worth coming for," boasted Trent. He opened the wooden storm shutters and stepped out onto a small narrow balcony. "In daylight hours, you can see one-hundred and eighty degrees of the Oasis from where I am standing. On the other side of the barn, you can see the other side of the Oasis."

Naomi stepped next to Trent. She looked skywards. The view took her breath away.

"The stars are beautiful," she managed to whisper. "There's no possible way you can count them."

"Three thousand one hundred and five, to be exact," insisted Trent.

Naomi's eyebrows angled to a point. "Don't tell me you've counted them?"

His grin stretched wider. "No, I'm kidding."

Naomi giggled. "I've never seen a more beautiful sight," she whispered.

"I have."

"Where?" she asked.

"I'm looking at her," hinted Trent.

Naomi didn't remove her gaze from the view. Her cheeks reddened. Her entire body tingled at hearing his words. 'How on Earth could the love between them germinate into anything more than a feeling?' The question overlapped again and again inside her mind.

Trent stepped back. He held out his hand. "Care to dance?"

"There's no music."

"What if there was?"

"I'd think you were forfeiting the bet we made which means I'd win by default."

"I'm not concerned over the bet. I planned for you to win all along."

Trent pushed a button on the key ring. At first, nothing happened. His hand gently took Naomi by the chin. He gently lifted her head. For a short time, they looked at each other then he bowed gracefully.

"What are you up to Trent Stanton?"

A quiet romantic melody started to play from a speaker on the wall. The tune seemed to hover in the still night air. Naomi found herself slowly slipping into a hypnotic trance. Trent stepped closer to his dance partner. In silence, they started a slow waltz on the balcony under the countless stars.

Naomi felt she'd died and gone to heaven. Her mind closed the question on how everything could fit together or even work between her and Trent. She felt so light on her feet she thought she might be floating. Every road Naomi looked down in her mind led to love. She didn't try to hinder the idea. They were waltzing in the middle of Australia, in a barn full of hay, a place where she never expected to find happiness let alone love. She wanted the dance to last forever.

When the song ended, the two dancers kept swaying in time to the beating of their heart. Naomi gazed at Trent's eyes. They were wet just like hers. He lowered his head. Naomi stood on her toes. For the first time, their lips lightly touched. She leaned closer making their lips weld together. Electricity arced between them. The couple stopped swaying, locked in a long passionate, romantic kiss.

The spark of love quickly roared into a raging fire.

Trent's hand easily undid the dressing gown. Naomi, felt it fall to her feet.

"Excuse me. Sorry for disturbing the moment." The whispered voice sounded so quiet the two lovebirds nearly missed the interruption.

Trent looked sideways towards the trap door. Naomi squealed, sprinting to the edge of the balcony.

"Mother!" remarked Trent. He didn't sound upset or surprised.

"Your father sent me to find you. He has an urgent message."

"How did you know we'd be here?"

"Where else could my son take a young lady for some privacy?"

"I'm glad Earl didn't come here," whispered Naomi, swiping the dressing gown from off the floor.

"Believe me; I almost didn't convince him to stay in the house."

"Thanks," said Trent.

"So much for a place where we won't be disturbed," moaned Naomi, raising her eyebrows.

"Earl told me he didn't have a choice. He needs your help," said Margaret.

CHAPTER THIRTEEN

MARGARET STANTON led her son and Naomi back to the house and to the study room.

Along one wall Naomi saw computer paper stacked neatly at least half a metre high in ten different piles. A wooden three drawer filing cabinet occupied one corner. The cabinet looked as though it hadn't been opened in years.

"The office seems to be a nice place to sit and reflect," said Naomi, waving her hand in the air. "Dare I say the whole of the Oasis seems a nice place to sit and reflect? Maybe that's the trouble. Everyone's too relaxed. The great Australian saying, 'she'll be right. Tomorrow is another day,' is too frivolous a saying." She walked to the desk, turning her nose up. "Please tell me the piles of papers are in year order."

Earl Stanton stepped away from the window, glaring at his wife. He looked sideways at Naomi.

"Yes, they are."

"You just saved me six months of work," advised Naomi on a sigh.

Earl Stanton's brow formed deep wrinkles. "I'll have you know my wife and I disagree on her idea I should allow you the privilege of snooping through my paperwork."

"I thought your wife said it'd be okay?"

"Please, let me finish. She helped to convince me to see the light of day. Perhaps you were the miracle I've been praying for?"

"I'll do my best."

"I suppose a thank you is in order. If there's anything I can do to help, please feel free to let me know?" The big man marched across the room and stood next to his son.

"You and Trent can leave me alone. You have helped enough," advised Naomi.

"Come on you two," insisted Margaret Stanton. "Let's leave the young lady to her work." She ushered Trent and her husband out of the room, clicking the door shut.

"You know I don't like anyone poking their nose in the books," grumbled Stanton staring nervously at his wife.

"Darling, you agreed you don't have much of a choice." Margaret took hold of her husband's arm. Holding him tight, she dragged him away from the room. "She'll be right."

Naomi marched across the floor to the door. She was in time to hear the group walk away. A muffled conversation coming from the dining room forced her to open the door a tad. Unable to understand the conversation, Naomi closed the study door and strolled across the room and sat in the black leather chair.

"I believe this chair may be a tax deduction," she mumbled. After searching the antique mahogany desk for paper and pen, Naomi gazed around the room noting there were books from floor to ceiling. "Someone's stacked these books in alphabetical order," she whispered, running her fingers horizontally across the spine of at least two hundred books. "A place for everything; and everything in its rightful place," she stated. Grinning, she sat back at the desk.

Naomi worked tirelessly through the night. At 2:00am Trent opened the door.

"Can I get you anything?" he asked.

Naomi looked up. "A mug of hot coffee will be lovely."

Trent disappeared. In minutes, he returned carrying a mug of hot brew.

"Thank you, now please leave."

At 3:00am Trent again pushed his head through the open door.

"Coffee?" he whispered tentatively.

Naomi grinned. "Thank you."

She kept glancing at the clock waiting for Trent's return. To help pass the time, she walked to the window, pulling open the heavy gold crested drapes. She could barely see the barn where she and Trent had waltzed to the melody of the romantic song.

On a sigh, Naomi wrapped her arms around her waist. She could still hear the music in her mind. Humming softly to herself, she closed her eyes. Her imagination easily took her back to the barn where Trent had asked her to dance. She began to sway, lost in her imagination.

"Do we have a future together?" she questioned.

"I hope we do."

The voice broke through Naomi's fantasy, making her jolt. She opened her eyes as an arm slipped around her waist. She turned and looked directly at Trent. The expression on his face made her knees buckle. Her heart pounded against her rib cage. She took a step back in a desperate bid to regain control.

Trent stepped forward.

"Stay away," she warned.

"Please, don't stop what you were thinking."

"I don't know what you mean?" Naomi brushed past him on her way back to the desk.

Trent grabbed her arm, sweeping her in close. He kissed her passionately.

Even if Naomi could, she didn't pull away. She wanted Trent and groped for his shoulders when he lifted her in his arms.

"If you keep this up, I won't want you to leave," she taunted.

"I don't want to go."

"You have to. I'm not finished going through the books."

Trent turned her around so he could massage her neck.

"You have magic hands," Naomi whispered.

Trent kissed the back of her neck.

"Don't." Naomi's protest sounded mild at best.

"Why not?" asked Trent.

"I'll force you to stay."

"Good. How's everything looking?"

"Fine," she answered, walking back to the chair. "I've only gone back one year. Already I've found twelve thousand dollars."

"How?" asked Trent.

"The fuel for the plane is a good place to begin. There's also the depreciation amount. How long have you owned the plane?"

"Two years."

"What did you use before?"

"We ran two choppers."

"Do you still have the helicopters?"

"Yes."

"Are they in good working condition?"

"Yes, we use them all the time."

"Does your father have a sore back?"

"No."

"Does he spend a lot of time sitting at the desk working?"

"Does it matter?" asked Trent.

"It does if you want to save the Oasis. The comfortable chair might be a tax deduction."

"My entire family does what they can."

"Forget it. Not worth the hassle."

Trent flicked through the seven hundred standard size papers sitting neatly on the desktop. He let out a low whistle.

"Tell me you don't have to work through each of those pages."

"I do." Naomi chuckled at his shocked expression. "It won't take long."

"Is there anything I can do?"

Naomi dug her nose out of a fuel bill. "You're doing everything you can."

"I'm not doing anything."

"Yes, you are. You're here in the same room as me."

Trent watched Naomi sort through page after page. She glanced up every few minutes to make sure he hadn't fallen asleep.

The cowboy watched her closely, observing anything she did.

Every time Naomi stretched; Trent would massage her shoulders. Whenever a rogue page accidentally fell to the floor, Trent picked it up.

After the third sheet of paper fell to the floor, Naomi started to play games by stepping on the paper.

"Love games using a piece of paper," chuckled Trent.

Naomi scrunched a page and threw it. She laughed when it hit him in the nose. Trent sprinted across the room to her chair, wrestling her to the floor. Almost immediately the tackle ended in a passionate kiss.

Earl Stanton barged into the room. "I heard a noise, is everything okay?"

"Yes, everything's fine," yelped Trent, jumping to a standing position.

Stanton shook his head and closed the door, leaving the two chuckling.

By 4:00am Naomi threw her pen down. She stretched her cramped muscles. She walked to the window, staring into the darkness at nothing in particular. Trent walked across the room and stood next to her.

"I'd love a cup of coffee."

Trent started sprinting for the study door before she finished her sentence. Naomi giggled at her sudden power.

By 4:45am Naomi reached for the phone. She dialed her home phone.

"Hello," croaked a voice on the seventh ring.

"Kaite, sorry to wake you, I have an urgent task for you to complete."

Her best friend groped for the bedside clock. "Naomi, do you know what time it is?"

"Yes, I do."

"The numbers on my alarm clock are a blur. If I may add, the sun is not up yet. Why the urgent call? Couldn't it wait until the rooster made a noise?"

"I wanted to call you long before the rooster was awake. Though I thought I heard it crow five minutes ago."

"You are not making any sense. Call me back later."

"Kaite, wake up. I need your help. I've also got news for you."

Naomi's flat-mate struggled to a sitting position. "Do you know what time I got to bed this morning?"

"Knowing you; probably five minutes before I rang."

"Almost correct," grumbled Kaite. "Twelve minutes ago."

"Sorry, my timing was slightly off. I thought you might have just got home."

"You made a lousy guess."

"Kaite, are you awake yet?"

"Yes, I'm awake," she answered in a voice that still sounded asleep.

"I met this wonderful bloke."

"Good for you. Now can I go back to bed?"

"No."

"Please."

"Kaite, Trent has a handsome brother a tad younger than you."

"Who's Trent?"

"It's a long story."

"Ok, I'm fully awake. I'm listening."

By the time, Naomi relayed to Kaite the general idea about Trent, his brother Mitch and the Oasis, her best friend started doing seat drops on the edge of the bed.

"I haven't mentioned the best part," hinted Naomi.

"Tell me more," begged Kaite.

"What would you say if I can con Earl Stanton into flying you out here to the Oasis in a helicopter?"

"I'd say yes. Will he do it?"

"I'm certain of it. Even if you and Mitch don't hit it off, the short holiday will help you to feel revitalized. Wear something comfortable. You need to ride a horse."

Kaite screamed in excitement. "I've never kissed a cowboy."

"There's one thing you have to do for me. Open my briefcase, find the tax sheet and fax it to me."

"The one Brandt gave you to keep safe?"

"Yes."

"I don't have your combination to the briefcase."

"5541."

"You want me to burn it?"

"I want you to fax it to me."

"You're going to send it to Brandt's clients to get him into trouble? Great plan Naomi. He is going to be pissed."

"Kaite, please, this is important. I'll text you the fax phone number of where I am. After you've faxed the form put it back exactly where you found it."

"Okay, I'll do it even though I don't understand what you're up to."

"After you've done it, pack a small suitcase. Wait by the phone for a call from Earl Stanton."

Kaite replaced the phone on its hook and bounded across the room. She found the briefcase, tapped in the code then walked across the room to the fax machine. She waited for the fax machine to deliver the message, replaced the paper in the briefcase and went back to bed.

CHAPTER FOURTEEN

THE MOON quickly disappeared to the opposite side of the world. The sun started to shine on a brand-new day when Naomi finally dug her nose from the computer screen and looked over the top of the monitor. She watched Trent sneaking into the room and placing two coffee mugs on the desk. Quieter than a fox stalking chickens, he settled himself down in a black leather recliner. Gazing at the man, Naomi knew she'd fallen in love. Trent flashed his natural smile, making her knees go to jelly. Naomi marveled again at his handsome, tanned face, his boyish looks. She sighed and returned her attention to the computer.

"I didn't know if I should talk," quipped Trent.

Naomi giggled, hunching further over the computer keyboard. She giggled again when the fax machine whirred to life.

"Be a darling, fetch the faxed paper."

Trent walked over to a small table by the window. He watched the paper being spat out of the machine. He grabbed it as it fell to the floor.

"The name on this paper isn't Earl Stanton."

Naomi collected the paper from his hand. "It soon will be."

Trent watched her erase the name and the numbers on the sheet, replacing them with the name Stanton and lots of numbers.

Finally, Naomi walked over to the fax machine, entering the numbers to the tax office. She stood smiling, watching the paper disappear and reappear. She relayed in an authoritative voice, "done."

Trent stepped up for a kiss.

Naomi gave him a peck on the cheek, walking back to the desk. She stacked the papers neatly, slipping them into individual manila folders.

"Where's my proper kiss?" asked Trent, his voice sounding hurt.

"Not yet. When I have stored these papers in the old cabinet, I can relax."

Holding the piles of folders, Naomi knelt on the floor, opening the bottom drawer too far. The drawer fell on to the carpet, revealing yellow papers.

"Those old papers must have fallen at the back of the drawer years ago," announced Trent marching over.

Naomi scooped up the yellowing pile, walked over to the desk, and placed the wrinkled papers in a neat pile, ironing each one flat using the palm of her hand.

"This first paper is a legal document from the year 1898."

Trent bent forward over the paper. "It states here in the middle of the page the government of the Northern Territory will freely give to the Stanton name all that is discovered in the middle of the desert. It also states the Oasis has been freely given to the Stanton family." He looked up. "It's great news."

Naomi dropped her gaze and read the remainder of the legal document.

"The name of the Governor of the time I can't read, however, the stamp is official. The last part is hard to decipher. It states; free from any form of tax is awarded to the Stanton family and the land named 'The Oasis' for the valuable, unselfish act the Stanton's provided during the first world war. The Stanton's have gone above their duty. For this reason, we the government will not charge a tax of any sort or description to the Stanton family for the next three hundred years."

Trent and Naomi looked at each other in silence. Trent eventually was the first to respond to the news. He reached out, hugging Naomi. Picking her up, he carried her to the outside swing. A rooster crowed. A fox darted past them on its journey home.

In the fresh air, the love birds kissed. Naomi felt happier than she ever dreamed. She certainly wasn't going to be the first to disturb their romantic moment.

Earl Stanton stepped out onto the verandah. He stretched in the early morning air. Studying the area, he nodded. He waved at a blue heeler. Stanton watched the dog chase the black bull away from the cattle grid.

Trent surfaced, grinning.

"Nice morning. I can feel it in me bones this will be a good day," called Earl.

His son looked puzzled. "How did you know?"

"Naomi visited me at around four this morning. I'd been pacing the floor waiting to hear news on the fate of the Oasis. You should have seen her face when I spoke from the corner of the room. I swear her feet left the floor." He chuckled a little. "She told you the news?"

"Yes," answered Trent.

"Miss Naomi Genius, not only did you save the Oasis, we have enough surplus money to buy Davey's farm and his five hundred head of cattle. I've been on the blower already to seal the deal. He told me to take the cows whenever I'm ready. He's also agreed to sell me his land."

"You've been wanting his farm for ten years. Why does he want to sell to us now? He doesn't like us," said Trent.

"He doesn't care who gives him the money. He just doesn't want the government to get their hands on his land."

Trent nodded.

"I offered him a job at the Oasis," added Stanton.

"Dad, what about Naomi, she should have the vacancy?"

"I've offered her a special job."

Trent swept a puzzled look between Naomi and his father. "What have you cooked up between you?"

"I offered your father a deal he couldn't refuse." Naomi raised her eyebrows, her face breaking out into a widening grin.

Stanton walked over to the swing. "It's true. I've employed Naomi to be our official tax accountant."

"What about the Jillaroo job?" Trent asked.

"I don't think so. Naomi's figure is too shapely."

Naomi's face flushed red with embarrassment.

Earl pointed his finger at his son. "Trent, if you upset this young woman in any way, you and I will have words. Get the picture?"

Trent flashed his father the famous Stanton nod.

"Excuse me, Sir," interrupted Naomi.

"Please, call me Earl."

"You haven't heard the best news."

"What could be better than what you've told me?" He winked. "Let me guess. You two want to get married?"

Margaret stepped onto the verandah in time to hear the word, 'married.' She clasped her hands together, sprinting over to be by her husband's side.

"Mum, Dad, it's not what the news is about," corrected Trent.

"If it's not the news, I think you should inform me?" said Earl.

Naomi showed him the official government form. Stanton held it in trembling hands. He read it through twice before starting to dance. His feet stirred up the drying ground.

"What's the news?" asked Margaret, reaching out for the yellow page.

Earl handed her the letter and continued to dance. After reading the handwritten note, Margaret joined her husband, Trent, and Naomi in a group dance.

"Not only did you save the Oasis by finding the fifty thousand dollars, you found the letter. It's been missing for the past ten years. The government didn't accept what I've been trying to tell them. They believe I'm so desperate to save my land, I made up the rumor of a land tax pardon. I can now go to the government, demanding they pay me two hundred thousand dollars they've taken off me in back taxes over the years to sweep me from this land." Earl danced towards the house, consumed in the excitement. He disappeared inside the house only to march back to the swing carrying four plates of bacon and eggs. "Great job, Naomi. Come, everyone, sit on a swing. Let's eat breakfast together."

"Thanks, Earl," chirped Naomi. "Are you going to tell the remainder of your family?"

"I will when they arrive here for breakfast. Until then, this moment belongs to us four. How do you feel about a small roundup? I don't want Davey to suddenly change his mind."

Naomi's eyes sparkled at thinking about the upcoming cattle muster. "Sounds like a job a city girl can't turn her nose up at."

When the small group had finished breakfast, Earl collected the bacon scraps.

"Watch what happens when I clap my hands," Trent said.

When Naomi heard thud after thud hitting the polished verandah boards her eyes widened in fear. She watched the commotion of six blue heeler dogs swirling around Trent. Twelve excited eyes glanced her way.

"Sit!" commanded Trent.

Earl stood, staring at the dogs. They scampered from Trent's side, jumping for the bacon.

"Down the lot of you," Stanton ordered.

Six backsides hit the deck.

"Well trained dogs," laughed Naomi.

"Don't be fooled over their shenanigans. They do exactly what they're trained to do," explained Earl.

"Especially when they're about to eat a small meal of bacon," added Trent.

"What are they trained for?"

"They round up cattle."

Naomi's expression portrayed a woman who looked full of doubt.

"I'll prove it," boasted Trent.

Earl looked over, grinning at Naomi's disbelief.

Trent whistled twice. Six dogs stood, giving him their full attention. He created three sharp whistles. The dogs sat as one. Trent grinned mischievously. "If I make four sharp whistles, they attack." He stuck three fingers in his mouth.

Naomi tried to swallow the lump in her throat as she counted each of his four whistles. The dogs turned their head and stared at her. Naomi stepped back. The dogs ran towards her. She screamed, climbing the swing. Twenty-four paws came running at full tilt, surrounding Trent. He and Earl fell on to a swing laughing uncontrollably.

"Trent, you tricked me. I am not amused."

Earl and Trent instantly ceased laughing. His next whistle saw the dogs run off. Trent scooped Naomi into his arms and kissed her anger away.

"Sorry, I played a bush joke. The dogs wouldn't hurt Charlie let alone attack. They were confused over the four whistles. The dogs probably thought they were about to get more bacon to eat."

Using a casual swipe of her hand, Naomi lovingly slapped Trent's face. Leaning in, she kissed his cheek.

Earl cleared his throat. "Come on you two; we have a job to do. By the time we arrive at Davey's farm, I mean, my farm, it'll be midmorning."

Inside twenty minutes Trent's brothers were fetched, the horses were saddled, and the motorbikes had been fuelled. Trent whistled. The dogs sprinted back. After Trent relayed the good news to his brothers, they roared, throwing their wide-brimmed hat high into the air. The dogs chorused by barking.

Naomi watched Trent's family kiss each other goodbye. Riding their horse, the group followed Earl in pairs towards a narrow path which led to the vertical wall that encompassed the Oasis.

By the time the group reached the base of the vertical cliff, Naomi felt comfortable sitting on the back of a black horse. His name was Ben. Trent rode a fit ex-racehorse. Its nickname was Tiger. Glancing at the sky, Naomi stared at the clouds moving at speed and disappear over the wall.

The trail leading to the top looked narrow. For the first few minutes, Naomi kept her stare locked on the cliff face, too frightened to look at the shrinking base. She felt amazed at how easily her horse could stay in the middle of the sheep track. She surmised it had completed ascending and descending the wall many times. Eventually, she summoned enough willpower to glance at the aerial view of the Oasis. The scene from the plane didn't give the oval shaped hole in the ground justice. She wanted to stop her horse just to stare at the serenity and the actual size of the place. The vivid colors in the walls from the top to the base of the Oasis were captivating. Naomi even spied a rainbow stretching the width of the oval shaped canyon.

"I did mention to you this place is magnificent," declared Trent, from behind.

Naomi swiveled on her saddle, smiling at the man staring at her. He'd unclipped his rope and looked more than ready to use it.

"What's wrong?"

"I have the rope ready just in case someone falls off the side."

A warm feeling flowed through Naomi's body from her feet to her head. Trent, her knight in shining armor, seemed almost faultless. The only thing lacking was the perfect gift. She faced the way they were travelling, pondering if he could ever discover it. Inwardly she contemplated the question.

'Was it essential for Trent to discover the perfect gift?'

CHAPTER FIFTEEN

THE ASCENT of the almost vertical wall of the Oasis took fifteen minutes. At the top, the riders dismounted. They grouped together for a hot coffee while the horses and the dogs took a well-earned rest.

"The coffee smells nice," chirped Naomi, holding her mug out.

Trent immediately filled it.

The temperature felt as though it had dropped, causing Naomi to shiver. For warmth, she wrapped her fingers tight around the mug of hot brew.

"It's the coldest before the dawn. As yet the temperature has failed to increase," explained Trent. Lifting his gaze skywards, he quickly added. "It'll be raining soon."

"How can you tell?"

"We call Trent the walking weatherman," declared Earl.

"Is he ever wrong?"

"Let me think. He probably has been a couple of times. When, I can't remember," moaned Stanton.

"Out here the temperature can plummet up to seven degrees in minutes," advised Mitch.

Naomi shivered again. With the mug to her lips, she swallowed a mouthful of coffee. She relished in the warmth of the liquid sliding down her throat.

Trent stared closely at the horizon. His gaze seemed fixed on a group of small clouds floating towards them.

"Don't tell me, the clouds talk to you?" giggled Naomi, digging Trent in the ribs.

"No, they don't talk. I have to stress it is going to rain very soon."

Naomi studied the sky. "They look like harmless fluffy white clouds to me."

"Don't be fooled. I predict it's going to rain in two hours, the same as yesterday."

Earl stood. "Boys, mount up. It's time to go."

Stanton's family packed everything, mounting their horse inside two minutes.

A small derelict cottage came into view after thirty minutes of riding. Beyond the cottage, Naomi saw five-hundred skinny head of cattle grazing on what they could find growing in the dust. She immediately felt sorry for the beasts.

"We came for them," said Trent, pointing to the cattle.

A man and a woman, both about Trent's age, stepped out of the cottage. The young man held a .22 rifle in his right hand. When he recognized the faces in the group, he pointed the rifle at the ground.

Earl dismounted his horse and marched towards the house.

"Trent, what's the meaning of the posse?" questioned the woman, folding her arms. "Earl Stanton, stop right where you are, you know you're not welcome here."

"Dad, let me handle this," called Trent.

His father nodded and walked back to his horse.

"Mary-Lou, we need to have a short talk. The clock's ticking."

"You betcha it's ticking," snarled Mary-Lou.

"I'll make the explanation short. The storm is on her way."

"You have five seconds to tell me the reason for your visit. If you don't, there's going to be a bullet in your head."

"Are you still holding a grudge? It's been years."

"Sure am."

Naomi frowned. "This woman is your ex-girlfriend?"

Trent slowly nodded.

Mary-Lou sniffed the air, pointing a long slender finger at Naomi. The wind suddenly blew up, ruffling the country woman's long blonde hair. She brushed it to one side letting the wind take charge.

"You smell like a city chic. Take my advice, turn around, go back where you came from. You don't belong out here."

"How can you know I came from the city?"

"You have the word 'city' written on your pretty little face." She boasted a sarcastic smirk. "Stinking city girls can't cut it out here."

"Mary-Lou, enough," said Trent. "Where's Roy? We've come for the cows."

"Over my dead body," she hissed.

"I hope it won't come to that."

"Always the gentleman, Eh! Trent?" taunted Mary-Lou, spitting on the ground. "Pop, get your arse out here."

Roy came staggering out of the cottage, leaning his drunken frame against a wooden verandah post. "Mary-Lou, shut up and get in the house. These fine people are here for the cows."

"You got a copy of the legal papers?"

"There aren't any. It's a gentlemen's agreement," boasted Roy.

"A what?" Mary-Lou snorted.

"It's been agreed the Stanton's will take the cows, the house and the land for a dollar."

"Never! I won't allow it." Mary-Lou snatched the rifle from Henry and pointed it at Trent.

"Put the rifle down," yelled Roy. "They have to take the cows before it's too late. The trucks the bank has hired will be here tomorrow morning. They're going to sell this place from under me for whatever they can unless everything is settled between us right now. I'd rather sell to the Stanton's than have the bank take everything."

Mary-Lou sank to her knees and sobbed. "Where are we to go?"

"We've received a couple of good offers for work," said Roy.

Naomi walked over, placing her arm around Mary-Lou. She stood, giving her a mighty push. Trent scooped Naomi up in his arms before she hit the dirt.

"Nice catch. I remember you doing the same thing for me once." Mary-Lou turned away from group and sprinted into the house.

"Thanks," said Naomi.

"The pleasure is all mine," replied Trent.

"You should go talk to Mary-Lou."

"Are you sure?"

"I trust you," said Naomi.

Trent kissed her, nodded and marched boldly into the house.

"Mary-Lou, where are you?"

He searched the house, stopping at a closed bedroom door. He knocked like a gentleman should.

"Enter," whimpered a sobbing voice.

Trent opened the door. Leaning casually against the door frame, he refused Mary-Lou's offer to enter the room.

"Do you love the city girl?" questioned Mary-Lou.

"Her name is Naomi. Yes, I do."

"Does this mean there's no, 'us'?"

Trent rolled his eyes. "There has never been anything between us. Not since you called our relationship off when we were both sixteen."

"Do you call it nothing when you came from the Oasis to see me for breakfast before my father made us move to this place?"

"I have to admit, I did love you more than life."

Mary-Lou stood square to Trent. She held her arms open. "Come here and kiss me."

"I don't think so," jeered Trent. He shook his head.

"I've regretted not running after you from the moment you left."

"It's been a long time. I've grown up."

"I won't give up on us until you say I do at the altar. You have to make a choice. It's the city girl or me?"

Trent marched out of the house, never looking back.

Naomi noticed his deliberate walk. His speed didn't falter from the door of the house to his horse.

Mary-Lou leaned out of her bedroom window. "Trent, darling, make your mind up. It's me or her?"

"Dad, it's time to go. The storm has almost arrived. Let's get these cows home."

Trent smiled lovingly at Naomi, tipping his wide-brimmed hat. Without any further delay, the group galloped off towards the herd.

Naomi copied what the group did and brought up the rear.

The dogs ran around barking at the cattle, helping to gather the herd in close. The cows mooed, the dogs barked, Trent, his brothers, and their father waved their wide-brimmed hat in the air, shouting. Naomi heard the occasional whip crack. Trent grinned at the new Jillaroo as she took up her position on the left flank amongst the swirling dust.

Naomi glanced at the sky. She saw the black clouds bearing down on the group. She looked for Trent who returned a sharp nod. She faked a grin, amazed at his calmness. She saw him wave a hand in the air. Then she heard another whip crack.

The cows were on the move.

For a few minutes, Naomi looked lost in the fantasy world of a western movie. She boasted a grin at the sudden power over the half-starved beasts.

Through the swirling dust the cows were slowly pushed along towards the Oasis.

Naomi heard Trent whistle. The dogs barked louder at the lead cow. Their pace slowly increased. Naomi let go of a huge sigh. At last, they were heading for the Oasis at a reasonable speed.

A cow strayed from the 500 head, making a beeline for Naomi's horse. In the distance, she heard the scream of a motorbike. One of the dogs barked. The cow bumped into Naomi's horse, flinging her sideways. By some miracle, she managed to grip the saddle. She had almost corrected the precarious angle she found herself in when the strengthening wind flew dust into her eyes. She screamed at the stinging sensation. She felt her grip weakening when something pushed her upright so she could sit high in the saddle. Finally wiping the dust from her eyes, Naomi saw Mary-Lou's weathered face.

Trent finally burst through the herd, his rope at the ready.

"You should keep an eye on the city chick," spat Mary-Lou. Roaring away, she was instantly swallowed by the dust.

"I'd almost made it here," whimpered Trent, re-clipping the rope back on to his belt.

"I know. If I can make a suggestion, I'm more of an expert on a bike."

Trent whistled at Mitch.

Standing on the seat of the bike he momentarily split the herd of cattle by speeding up to Trent. He followed up with a few doughnuts in the dirt. When the bike dropped to idle, he grinned at Naomi's serious expression.

"Mitch, I need you and Naomi to swap. She's having a bit of trouble staying on the horse in this wind. If we want to beat the storm, we have to pick up a lot more pace."

The leather saddle squeaked when Naomi slid to the ground. A small dust cloud erupted around her ankles. In seconds the wind had dispersed the dust into the air.

Trent saw lightning fork across the sky. The familiar clap of thunder soon followed.

Mitch nodded. He displayed a knowing expression as he galloped away. Naomi couldn't comprehend the silent communication each member of the Stanton family seemed to have mastered. She secretly wondered if she could eventually master the silent nod too.

"Go," Naomi whispered to Trent. "Just like you, I've been looking at the sky. I'm no expert, I think the rain is ready to fall."

Trent motioned a sharp nod. He gave his horse a slight kick. Naomi felt the first rain drop fall. The she heard Trent's whip crack. The noise seemed to make the cows double their walking speed.

Overhead, the sky darkened further. The wind gusts intensified. Naomi shielded her eyes from the stinging sand. The wind swung from a tail wind to a head wind when they changed to a more direct approach to the Oasis.

The dust thickened with each tick of the clock. Naomi caught a glimpse of Mitch at the front of the herd then she lost sight of him through the swirling dust. Even the cows seemed to be agitated at having to walk head first into the wind.

Naomi jumped on the motorbike. She twisted the accelerator throttle. The bike revved and shot off into the swirling dust. Whenever a cow strayed from the path, she'd smack its rump. Each beast she smacked seemed to get the message to stay in line.

The minutes quickly ticked off. The approaching storm seemed relentless in trying to scatter the skittish herd of cows.

Eventually, Naomi felt her strength starting to wane. Time and again she wondered how much further? Half an hour after they gathered up the herd, she needed to fight the idea they might be going in the wrong direction.

A figure on a horse loomed out of the dust. He appeared to be a silhouette against the flying dust.

Trent looked down, yelling over the wind. "We have about five minutes before the storm hits. At roughly the same time we'll be starting our descent into the Oasis."

Seeing Mitch galloping up, Naomi nodded. When Mitch pulled alongside his brother, both men portrayed a different look. Mitch glanced at Naomi, nodded and galloped off.

"What was meant by the nod?" asked Naomi.

"Mitch suggested we try to sprint the cows down into the Oasis. I told him if we pull off the stunt and only lose no more than ten cows it will be a miracle. Don't get me wrong; we don't want to lose a single cow if we can help it. I wouldn't want an animal to fall to its death when the Oasis is so close."

"You got an entire conversation from a look?"

Trent chuckled. "Not really. We've done this sort of thing too many times to count."

Mary-Lou, roared up on her bike. "Quit stalling; get these cows moving."

Trent tried to explain the situation. Mary-Lou snorted. She pulled a grotesque face and rode off into the wind.

Trent looked at Naomi's concerned expression. "She'll be okay. She needs some time alone. At least the cows will listen to her whining."

"Where do you want me?" asked Naomi, muffling a laugh.

"I want you first down the path. When it starts to rain, I want you safely on the ground, standing on the covered cattle grid counting the cows when they walk past."

Naomi roared off to join Mitch at the head of the herd. She loved every minute of suddenly feeling important. Brandt never made her feel important. He'd been a total loser. Feeling a warmth creep through her body, Naomi never dreamt of being out in the middle of Australia, riding a motorbike down a steep, narrow dirt path that led into the belly of a possible ancient meteorite site could be so thrilling. She felt proud at the thought of fitting in. Deep down she prayed Trent might seriously consider asking her to marry him. She'd finally given into her heart. Now she wanted to stay next to the cowboy who called himself Trent Stanton all her days.

Naomi slowly rode down the steep descent. When finally reaching the bottom, she felt a deep sense of relief. Stopping her bike next to the covered cattle grid, she switched the motor off and studied the sky.

Above the Oasis Trent also studied the sky. He cupped a hand around his mouth, yelling over the increasing wind. "Dad, if I can make a suggestion."

Earl Stanton made his horse trot over to his son.

"We have to get these cows down the cliff face sooner than later. It did enter my mind to get them back exactly where we found them. I think we'll lose the entire herd if we try. The idea Mitch said is sound. He thinks we should send the cows down in pairs."

Earl Stanton nodded. "You're right. If we don't risk the cows going down the track two at a time, we might lose the entire herd. Let's do it. Time is at an end."

Trent whistled for the dogs to keep the cattle moving while his brothers forced the cows to double up by poking them in the ribs. Under sufferance the cows came together to start their descent into the Oasis.

Naomi roamed her stare between the cows and the sky. The clouds looked angry. At any moment, they threatened to burst, dumping a torrent of water.

"If only the rain would hold off a little longer," Naomi mumbled.

The cows started to walk across the covered cattle grid in pairs and fan out to eat the luscious green grass. By the time, three hundred and fifty-seven cows had walked across the covered cattle grid the heavens opened. The raindrops were huge, crashing heavily at Naomi's feet. Overhead, the lightning slashed the sky. The deep rumble of thunder made her cringe.

"I hate thunderstorms," she mumbled, lifting the collar of her button up shirt.

The rain fell in torrents. Naomi's black eyelashes felt heavy when water glued the dust to the ends. Each strand of her hair dripped water and her clothes were wet through.

Mitch followed a dog down the cliff face, which in turn made the cattle ahead a little nervous. One of the bulls lost his footing, slipping perilously close to the edge. Naomi held her breath, watching the two-hundred-pound beast struggle to gain a good foothold.

"Four hundred and seventy-one," reported Naomi, when the bull finally walked over the cattle grid. She wanted to hug its large neck. When the bull looked at her through its black eyes, Naomi decided the idea might make him more irate.

Naomi looked up the cliff face. She shielded her eyes from the rain using her hands. "Mitch, why have the remainder of the cattle stopped?"

"They're probably starting to get a little agro. I think Trent has slowed them down. Dad's leading the others single file. If you study the track, it's looking too slippery for two cows at a time. Up to now, we've done well. Not one beast has fallen."

Naomi felt sick to the stomach at the idea of seeing a single cow falling to its death.

Mitch winked at her. "Don't worry. She'll be right."

Naomi raised an eyebrow at the comment. She could do nothing except wait patiently for the remainder of the herd to walk past her.

The rain poured down the path, turning it into a water slide. The fast-flowing river looked to have risen substantially, covering the mouth of the tunnel. The river seemed far worse than when she fell into it. Naomi grimaced at the thought of falling in again.

Lightning and thunder rolled together across the sky. The storm seemed to be hovering, determined to wash the Oasis from the Australian map.

Naomi stood square to Earl Stanton. "I've counted four hundred and ninety-nine cows. We only lost one." Glancing about the landscape, she looked directly at Mitch. "Where is Trent?"

"Everyone is here," replied Earl Stanton. "He must have gone ahead; everyone back to the house."

The group rode off in the direction of the mansion, scattering the newly formed congregation as they slowly mixed with the original herd.

Naomi hesitated long enough to decide Trent must still be on the plateau above the Oasis. She revved her motorbike to screaming pitch and tore up the slippery, narrow trail. She surfaced from out of the crater to find the countryside awash. The rain resembled a wall of grey.

Naomi blinked rapidly to help disperse the growing number of water droplets clinging to her eyelashes.

"What a transformation," she moaned.

In several places lightning split the dark sky. Thunder shook the ground under her feet. Naomi studied the surrounding water covered desert. Two shapes were standing in the rain at the edge of her sight. They came together and fell to the ground. Naomi gunned the bike's throttle fully open, roaring towards them. Mud sprayed out behind her in a thick sludge. The flooding plain forced her to do doughnuts in the mud in an attempt to keep the bike moving forward.

"Stop," she yelled. "Please stop."

Both men were wrestling in the mud. They couldn't hear her feeble attempts to make them quit. Dropping the bike in the mud, Naomi ran towards them. She saw Henry push Trent's head further into a puddle trying to drown her hero. Naomi screamed. She curled her fingers into tight fists, ready to king-hit Henry. She raised her fists high into the air and waited for the perfect time to strike.

Trent pushed hard against the ground, managing to fling Henry off. He unclipped his rope, lassoing Henry when he sprinted at Trent for the final onslaught. He stumbled over the tightening rope about his ankles, hitting the mud face first.

"What's going on?" screamed Naomi.

"My mate Henry wanted the cows back," said Trent. "When I tried to explain the sale in more detail he didn't want to listen. I even told him he'd be given fifty dollars for each cow."

Henry sat in a puddle of water, glaring up at Trent.

A motorbike came roaring up. Mary-Lou jumped off and ran towards her brother. Twelve large steps from the bike she stumbled in a pothole full of water and sprawled face first into a shallow puddle. Before she came to a stop, she had slipped into unconsciousness.

Trent sprinted over, dragging her out of the water.

"Will she be, okay?" asked Naomi.

"I hope so." Trent pushed the wet, muddy hair from her face.

The cold drops of rain falling heavily on to Mary-Lou's face were enough to bring her back. She opened her eyes, screaming.

"My ankle," she sobbed.

"Her ankle looks broken," said Naomi, noting the precarious angle of her boot.

Trent used his mobile phone to dial the Oasis. A quick sharp conversation followed. He slipped the phone back into his pocket and reassured both girls help was on the way.

Trent and Naomi squatted over Mary-Lou in an attempt to shelter her from the rain. Naomi felt like a schoolgirl again. The second the teacher turned his back; the kids could talk using their own developed silent signals. Trent and his family appeared to have developed a unique one of their own.

Mary-Lou watched Trent and Naomi. Between sobs she shook her head, pouting. For the first time, her eyes sparkled. Nodding at the two lovebirds, they didn't see her widening smile. They certainly didn't hear her giggles.

The reverberating throbs of a helicopter flying slowly across the now inland sea burst through the downpour. The wind from the rotors swirled the rain.

"The helicopter is giving us a cold shower!" shrieked Naomi. She watched the craft's wheels sink into the mud.

"More like having your body peppered by hail," said Trent.

He picked up Mary-Lou and carried her over to the helicopter. Naomi helped to strap her into the seat then talked to Earl Stanton while Trent helped Henry in and closed the door.

The helicopter's rotors spun at breakneck speed, lifting the craft into the air.

"What did you whisper to my father?" asked Trent.

Naomi put her arms around his waist, hugging him tight. "Can't I have at least one secret?"

After watching the helicopter vanish into the rain, Naomi faced her cowboy.

"I thought something awful happened to you."

"She'll be right," he answered.

"How can you always say; 'she'll be right?'"

"Henry and I were in the middle of a friendly wrestle. Besides, I always look on the positive side of everything."

Naomi playfully slapped Trent on the shoulder. "You sound just like your brother."

"No way, he sounds exactly like me."

"I have some good news. I finished counting the cows. We only lost one."

Trent reached out to reel Naomi in.

'This time, the moment won't be interrupted,' thought Naomi.

Something hard bumped the pair, forcing them to fall into the mud. Trent cushioned Naomi's fall and glared up at the beast. It lowered its head.

"He's number five hundred." Trent scratched behind the young bull's ears.

Naomi and Trent watched him walk off.

"He won't go far. He's just looking for something to eat. I saw him wander off from the main herd. Henry jumped me before I could go find him."

"You told me it was a friendly wrestle?" said Naomi.

"Eventually," admitted Trent.

The two stood in the rain in a tight embrace looking at the eyes of the other. In a slick move, their lips were locked. To Naomi, they were standing in a bubble full of warm sunshine and not in the middle of a storm.

CHAPTER SIXTEEN

THE NEXT day the sun rose in a cloudless sky. The rain had disappeared overnight. Naomi stretched in the warming rays of a new day. A few shallow, isolated puddles of water remained; the only evidence of the previous day's storm. Trent stepped out onto the verandah. A floorboard creaked under his weight.

Naomi turned to face him. She felt pleased to have greeted the sun before the cowboy.

"Just because you were up early you somehow think it's a victory?"

"Yes, I do. I wanted to see the sunrise. You are correct, it sure is beautiful out here." Naomi squared herself to Trent. "What are you hiding behind your back?"

"Two steaming plates of bacon and eggs on perfectly toasted brown bread," he announced.

"How did you get things ready so fast? I saw you asleep on the couch when I walked by. I felt proud of myself for being awake ahead of you."

"I have to confess I did have some help. Mum heard you walking down the stairs. She thought she should wake me. Together we made breakfast."

"What a cheat."

Naomi took the plate. She felt as though time had travelled backwards overnight, helping her to arrive at a school camp. She believed if she pinched herself, she might wake from her dream.

"For a city girl, you did a great job yesterday. I didn't know you could ride a dirt bike. You're a natural rider."

"Thank you for the compliment. My brother taught me how to ride. He refused to hear the word no. He even bought me lessons so we could ride together."

"I'd love to meet the man."

"My brother and a mate were sitting in the back of a car when it ran off the road. I sold both bikes after he died. I never rode again until yesterday. I have to admit, I did enjoy the experience, though I've never ridden in a storm."

"Sorry to hear of the news."

"It's been many years since that day. Although the pain has gone, I still think of him. I believe you and my brother would have gotten on."

"After breakfast and you feel up to it, we can go for a ride to survey the herd."

"I'd love to," chirped Naomi.

When Trent and Naomi finished the last mouthful of their breakfast, Earl came trotting up on a black mare. He gripped the saddle using one hand, the other, he held the reins of another two horses.

"Who'd like to go for a ride to check on the new arrivals?"

Naomi felt excited, walking towards a horse. Trent helped her on to the saddle of a brown chestnut. The horse instantly pricked its ears backwards waiting for a command.

"I thought you might want to know I picked up the extra package you asked me to get after dropping Mary-Lou at the hospital," whispered Earl.

"Thank you." Naomi's eyes sparkled. She lifted her backside off the saddle looking around the area.

"The package is asleep," whispered Earl. "Mitch is pacing the floor waiting for her to wake. You city people are all the same. It must be the clean air."

Naomi looked at Trent's puzzled expression. "It's part of my secret," she said.

"Are you going to share it?"

"I'll tell you when the time is right." She gave her horse a light kick, taking off in a fast trot.

Trent needed to make his horse gallop to catch up.

"We have to check the herd," Naomi said to Trent when he drew level. She felt full of pride knowing she finally had her very own little secret.

Trent chuckled and led the way to a small rise about a twelve-minute ride on horseback from the mansion. The hill looked high enough to watch the entire herd grazing.

"They look none the worse for wear after their wet ordeal," gushed Naomi.

"They've settled in very nicely. I'm positive it won't be too long before the cows put on weight again."

Naomi's gaze scoured the huge property. She visualized staying to live out the remainder of her life in such an overwhelming place. She allowed her mind to float back to the city; back to the busy streets of Melbourne, the endless cafés, shops and restaurants, the nightlife and the street people. She exhaled a sigh. The sights of Melbourne were indeed wonderful. She paused on the thought, pondering which one seemed more appealing; busy Melbourne or the splendor and magic of the Oasis. The two were locked together for only a heartbeat. The Oasis had already won. Besides, Trent lived here.

Naomi pouted. She stared at the ground, sighing quietly, so her cowboy didn't know. 'What would Kaite think? The city held her in its vice-like grip. The Oasis didn't. Kaite seemed to be hooked more on the nightlife than her. If only, out here in the middle of the desert, Kaite might be inspired to stay. If not, she'd have to decide between the two. In her heart, she already decided which one must win.'

Two horses approaching from the house brought Naomi back to reality. Earl waved at the new arrivals.

Naomi faced the riders, grinning at the sight of one of the figures. "Kaite!" she squealed. She jumped from her horse and started running.

Trent sprinted after her.

They ran side by side down the undulating side of the hill while Earl Stanton remained on guard. He resembled a King on his hill.

Kaite sat straight backed on a white horse looking like a professional rider. She pulled hard on the reins. When the horse came to a complete stop, she slid off the brown leather saddle. Mitch leapt from his horse. His arms were wide, ready to catch her if she fell.

"I take it you've met Mitch," puffed Naomi, between breaths.

"I have. Mitch sat next to me waiting for the exact moment I woke. Before I could say a word, he walked out of the room. When the handsome cowboy returned, he carried a plate full of bacon and eggs."

"You two are definitely from the same pod," giggled Naomi, glancing sideways at Trent.

"We are."

"This is an amazing place. It takes your breath away!" squealed Kaite, turning in circles.

"Yes, it does. This wonderful man standing next to me is Trent. He's the one I talked to you about. Mitch is Trent's brother."

Kaite shook his hand. Mitch stared at his brother, beckoning him to follow. The girls watched the two men walk up on top of the low hill to have a talk. Earl trotted off to inspect a pregnant cow.

"Naomi, I love this place," yelped Kaite.

"It is amazing. I have to decide whether to stay here or have Trent take me back home. The jillaroo job was only for two weeks."

"The way you were talking, I thought you were going to stay?"

"I would love to, but I have to admit I'm not convinced Trent wants me in his life."

"Naomi, don't take this the wrong way. I want us to stay best of friends forever. Don't be a fool. You're too hung up on the idea the bloke has to give you the perfect gift. If Trent is half the man Mitch is, he's the catch of the century. Blokes like these two don't fall from the sky every day."

"You're already in love with Mitch?"

Kaite slipped a giggle.

"How can you be so quick?"

"Unlike you, I believe in love at first sight. The more I know, the more I want."

"Is there such a thing as love at first sight?" questioned Naomi.

"You better believe there is. Surely you loved Trent the moment you laid eyes on the man. Though I have to admit, Mitch is the better looker."

"You think?"

Both girls started to giggle. Naomi looked for the two men.

"Something's wrong," whispered Naomi, sprinting for the hill.

When the girls reached the top, they spied the two men on the other side, locked in a wrestling duel.

Both girls sprinted down the hill yelling to stop the fight.

Trent looked up. Mitch saw his chance and quickly pushed his brother flat on his back.

"What's this?" yelled Naomi.

Mitch rolled over and began to laugh.

"We had a friendly wrestle," explained Trent.

"Friendly wrestle my arse!" screamed Naomi.

"Honest truth. The rodeo is today. Mitch wanted to show me a few moves he thought up. He wanted to prove he's the wrestling champ of the outback."

"I will be one day," he winked.

"One day you probably will be."

"What's the Goss about a rodeo?" quizzed Kaite.

CHAPTER SEVENTEEN

EXACTLY THIRTY minutes flying time from the Oasis, the helicopter hovered above the treetops that surrounded the rodeo. Still sitting snug in her seat, Naomi watched the many families bustling through the main gate. Each person displayed an excited look.

Groups of people were walking around the dust-covered ground totally oblivious to the new arrivals. They were too busy unloading horses, cows, sheep and musical equipment from the many trucks.

Naomi looked towards the boulevard of amusement rides. They were placed parallel to each other in a long line not far from the main oval. Men started to gather in front of the shooting gallery while the young ladies watched on. Each boasted the same expectant look of receiving a prize from their husband or boyfriend.

At the same time, the wheels of the helicopter touched terra firma, the reverberating throb of the rotors slowed then fell silent. Trent, Naomi, Mitch, and Kaite squeezed out of the helicopter and marched towards the main arena.

The smell of sawdust and horse sweat hung heavy over the entire grounds.

The rodeo crowd appeared to be swelling by the minute. The sandy oval three hundred kilometers from Brisbane resembled a hive of activity.

"Brother, we'll catch you up later. Kaite and I are off to the lover's ride," said Mitch.

Trent nodded and escorted Naomi arm in arm towards a large white marquee. He signed his name on a white sheet of paper clipped to a board and placed it back on a large tree stump. He quickly checked the time everyone expected him to win the rodeo.

"Half an hour to kick off," Trent advised, looking sideways at Naomi. "Can I take you down side-show alley?"

Naomi nodded. She squeezed Trent's arm.

To get to side show alley, they needed to walk past the novelty rides.

"The start of the boulevard is for the kids," Trent teased. "I'll take you to where the cowboys show what they're made of."

They turned the corner at the end of the alley and walked towards the adult games.

"Hey Trent," yelled a man. He lifted a fat cigar and shoved it back into his mouth.

Naomi looked for the voice. She found a man with a big stomach leaning over a portable square table.

"Give a bloke a break, keep on walkin'. Every time you stop to play me dart game you almost send me broke."

Trent helped Naomi over a puddle of water by lifting her gently into the air.

"Show off," moaned the man.

"Andy, it's good to see you. How goes?" asked Trent.

Both men grabbed each other's hand. In a show of strength, they shook hands in the air. The stranger's arm trembled as he tried to win the air hand wrestle. Eventually, he conceded defeat.

"You win," puffed Andy. Pulling his hand free, he massaged his shoulder. "I swear one of these days you'll push me arm right off."

"Naomi, this is Andrew. We call him Andy. Don't be shocked at how he talks or his appearance. Under his external frame, he's a good bloke. If you want something, this is the man to ask."

"Nice to meet you," said Naomi. She displayed a doubtful expression.

"Hey, Trent, where did ya dig this doll up from? If I were to guess, this one's a city chick?"

"She is."

"Are you gonna marry this one?"

Trent stared at the man through narrow slits, whispering. "I have to discover her idea of the perfect gift."

Andy raised his hands, attempting to change the subject. "It sure is good to see you again old boy. Going for another win? This year will make it five in a row. It'll be an outback rodeo record if you win."

"I'll win."

"You're a bit cocky," said Naomi.

"Little lady, he'll win for sure," stated Andy.

"I'll warm up by trying the hammer game," said Trent.

"No, you won't. The last time ya' swung the hammer ya broke the bell at the top. You cost me a small fortune in lost revenue. If ya want to stay friends, move your arse away from me darts and hammer game." Seeing Naomi pouting, he lowered his gaze and kicked at a clump of dirt. "Okay, Trent, you have one shot, for the little lady. Do me a favour; hit the rubber stop using half strength."

Trent picked up the long-handled hammer. Placing it on his shoulder, he walked over to the game. By the time, he started to focus on what he expected to happen, a crowd of people at least ten deep were standing a short distance away.

"Don't you be bothered by the number of people watching Naomi from the city; the big gorilla always attracts a crowd."

Gripping the handle at the very end, Trent arched his back. The head of the long-handled hammer touched the ground.

"Here we go again. This is how he's broken me game three years runnin.' To relax before his bull ride, he throws a perfect game of darts. Every year it's the same thing." He closed his eyes. "I can't watch. This is too painful."

In one massive show of strength, Trent brought the hammer over his head, striking the rubber hard. The weight at the base of the game flew upwards like a rocket towards the bell at the top. Everyone around heard a mighty bang. When the weight fell back to the rubber stopper at ground level, the machine lights came crashing down after the bell.

"Thanks, Trent. You've busted me machine yet again. Next year I'm gonna fix the weight to the ground. I'll have fun seeing you try and fail."

Trent grinned, picking out a large stuffed dog.

Naomi proudly placed it under her arm. She reached out and squeezed his bicep.

"Keep walking along this lane, and I'll pay Andy for the machine," whispered Trent in Naomi's ear. The moment she strolled off; Trent slipped the man a pile of rolled up fifty-dollar notes. "This should cover the cost of a few years-worth of damage."

"Thanks, mate. If there's anythin' ya need let me know." Andy slapped Trent on the shoulder. "If you want my advice, hog tie the little lady to make sure she won't get away." He raised his bushy eyebrows to cement his comments.

"As a matter of interest, maybe you can help me. You're an all-knowing bloke. You've been around Australia."

"Many times, over the years," interrupted Andy. He looked over Trent's shoulder and spied Naomi looking at the 'throw the ring at the bottles game.' "You want a second opinion of the city chick?"

"I don't need anyone to tell me she's the most gorgeous woman who has ever walked this Earth," advised Trent.

"You haven't seen a picture of me wife."

"You don't have a wife."

"I dream about the perfect woman every night. What's your question?"

"Naomi talks about this so called, 'perfect gift.' Have you any idea what it could be?"

"Buddy, you need to get out more often. Go to the city, the big smoke. Go and mingle. Smell the nightlife."

"It's not the answer I hoped to hear."

"Let me give you some advice from a bloke who knows."

Trent turned his head and saw Naomi walking towards them. "Get to the point; she's almost here."

Andy lowered his voice to a decibel above a whisper. Trent nodded as Naomi stepped level with the two blokes.

"What were you two conversing?"

"Andy told me some good advice."

"I hope I've put your mind at ease?"

"Yes, and thanks, mate. I owe you one."

"One what?" asked Naomi.

"I'll tell you later." Trent winked at Naomi.

'Another secret,' thought Naomi. The word doubt flashed into her mind. No matter how hard she tried to sweep the letters away, they stayed. Her mind needed to convince her heart there couldn't be a future with Trent if he kept up the secrets. Although the Oasis is magnificent, her thoughts drifted back to the city, beckoning her to return. She needed to find Kaite to let her know she made a bad call in tricking her into coming. They needed to quickly leave.

Trent led the way to the main arena where a large bull had been prepared. Several men slapped Trent on the shoulder when he walked by.

"I have to get ready," advised Trent. He leaned forward, kissing Naomi. "I won't be long."

"I'll be here when you return with the trophy. Trent, be careful."

Naomi climbed the rugged wooden fence framing the small sand covered arena. Although she felt convinced this would be her last day, she certainly didn't want to see Trent hurt. She nodded at the cowboy, determining in her mind he'd always be a good friend. Maybe they could stay in touch via letters. They could even make the occasional phone call. She smiled awkwardly, cherishing the thought.

Trent nodded and trotted over to the bull pen, disappearing amongst the sea of faces.

Naomi watched the proceedings. The air felt electric. She could hardly control the excitement welling up inside her. Slowly her thoughts drifted back to Kaite. Did she make the correct decision in forcing her to come? Naomi felt more confused than ever. The mixed signals Trent sent added to her confusion, tearing her between the city and out here yet again. In her heart she knew staying was the best thing. The secrets Trent kept locked inside his head happened to be the reason for her doubts.

On the other side of the arena, a few helicopters landed. Naomi focused on the first craft. Its rotor blades seemed to whirl for a lot longer than the others. Two men and a woman stepped down onto the ground. They stood staring at the country folk. One man from the group signaled the others to stay. Naomi saw him march towards the games. She struggled to swallow her anxiety and jumped from the fence. She watched the man switch directions and make a beeline for the patch of dirt she stood on. Naomi moved away, mingling amongst the crowd.

"Look what the storm blew in," said a voice on her left.

Naomi whirled around, staring at the man.

"Whatever you do don't turn to jelly."

"Brandt, what are you doing here?"

"I tracked you down by keeping an eye on Kaite. I knew she'd eventually lead me to you. Enough chit chat, let's go for a walk."

"No. I'm staying right here," said Naomi.

Brandt pulled a snub nose handgun from his pocket, thrusting the end into Naomi's ribs.

"You won't shoot me. There are too many witnesses."

"I'm not stupid, Naomi darling. Kaite is here somewhere. We'll find her together. Be warned, I'll shoot her if you don't do exactly what I tell you. In fact, look who is coming. What a coincidence. Now I know where Kaite is, tell me, where's the boyfriend?" Pushing his gun harder against Naomi's ribs, he snarled. "Don't tell me, let me guess. He's not any run of the mill cowboy. He has to be a hero for you to take any interest. Let me see if I can spot him. I spy a man sitting on the back of a rather large bull. He has to be the hero. If you don't want to see a bullet in his head or Kaite's, I suggest you come quietly."

Naomi's shoulders sagged in agreement.

"Good girl. You were always an easy puppet. Now start walking."

Naomi's mind churned over dozens of ideas, trying to derive at a suitable solution to stop Brandt's obsession over her. If she couldn't find a way, she knew he'd never stop.

"I'll come peacefully if you'll allow me to watch Trent?"

"So, I am correct. The cowboy sitting on the large bull's back is the one. I guess I can wait a few more minutes. Besides, it might be fun seeing a man getting trampled by a raging bull."

Trent signaled the Judge he was ready. His facial expression changed to stone. A buzzer sounded. The gate opened. The bull sprinted out of the holding pen. No matter how hard the bull bucked, twisted and turned, Trent stayed seated on his back. When a buzzer sounded, Trent's grin couldn't have been any wider. Not only did he win the trophy, he had beaten the record he set the previous year. He jumped from the tiring bull, waving to the cheering crowd. He didn't even look to have broken out in a sweat.

While Trent made his way to the winner's circle, Brandt pulled Naomi off the side railing and forced her to walk towards the helicopter.

Trent spotted them walking away from the fence and quickly shadowed them.

"Whatever you do, don't take me down sideshow alley," ordered Naomi.

Brandt snickered. "You've been watching too many movies girl. You want us to skirt around the trouble spot. I'm not stupid. The boulevard of games is the way you want us to go. Sideshow alley is the safe way. Now turn down here. No one puts one over on me." Brandt leaned close to Naomi's ear. "Not even you, my little puppet."

"What do you want?"

"I thought you were a smart girl. All those wins in the courtroom and you never figured me out. What a loser."

"You didn't answer my question?"

"Keep moving. Don't try anything stupid. The next bullet in my gun has your name on it."

Naomi bravely stopped. For her hesitation, she received a shove in the shoulder blade.

"My little puppet, I'll let you in on a little secret. In my pocket I have a tax form you will fill out. After you have filled it out the curtain will come down on your life."

"I won't do it."

"If you resist, the boyfriend cops it. I'll slightly modify what I've said. There's a bullet for Kaite, the cowboy and you."

"What do you hope to achieve by using a single tax form?"

"It will do plenty. Over the course of the coming years, bogus names will be written on the top of each form, signed by you. Inside six years I'll have ten million dollars in the bank. I will be living the high life somewhere in the Bahamas."

"Greed, it's the only thing you wanted me for?"

"I'm impressed; you are a smart girl. Our conversation is terminated. Keep moving."

Nearing Andy's broken machine, Naomi looked at the big man. While he stared back, she nodded at Andy, hoping he would understand her plight.

The man didn't appear to respond and quickly went about his business fixing his machine.

Questions tore through Naomi's mind. Did Andy see her nod? If so, why didn't he understand her plight? Why didn't he respond? She lowered her gaze to the ground and kept walking.

The big man waited for the pair to complete their funeral march past his machine and turn left towards the open paddock. He downed his tools and started to follow.

"Walk to the nearest helicopter. I have a pilot ready to take us up to an altitude of one hundred and fifty metres."

"How do you know he's still waiting?" quizzed Naomi.

"I pay people to do exactly what I say."

"What happens when we arrive at the prescribed height?"

Brandt's expression changed to concrete. "We'll both find out how good you can fly?"

"If the pilot of the helicopter is Earl Stanton, he won't allow you to commit murder," spat Naomi.

"Calling your boss by his first name is beyond you. The middle of nowhere is taking the city air out of your veins. My little puppet, Naomi Fitzgerald, you're a city girl. You will die a city girl."

Naomi glanced at the mirror maze on her left. She spied two dark, distorted shapes. She felt positive one must be Andy, the other one she hoped was Trent. She received a second shove in the shoulder blade for slowing.

"Stop stalling," blurted Brandt.

Closing in on the stunt show set, Naomi saw a man climbing the ladder to the balcony of a makeshift hotel. Seconds later, she spied a big man step from a doorway. Naomi punched Brandt's wrist, sending the snub nose handgun into the dusty ground. She back stepped when his hand came up to slap her face. Andy stepped closer. Brandt stood square to Andy.

"So, this is the hero, a three-hundred-pound blob of lard."

"Fella, I'm only two hundred and twenty pounds. I'm no hero. I see myself as Naomi's big brother."

A shadow dashed to Andy's side. "Thanks, big fella. I can take it from here."

"Another hero has arrived. If you want a piece of me, come and get it."

"Be careful Mitch, he knows Judo," screamed Naomi, from a doorway on the opposite side of the street.

"I know a few Japanese too. Nice people the lot."

Mitch stepped forward, pulling the first punch. Brandt kicked out, sending his opponent into the mud. Mitch quickly stood and readied himself for the next round.

A sharp whistle came from Trent. Everyone stopped and watched Trent complete a dive through the window of the fake saloon, complete a tumble roll in the dirt and stand to full height in front of Brandt.

"Three heroes on to one. I think it's fair," he spat.

Trent unbuckled his rope.

"You're going to tie me up so you can pulverize me into the ground?"

"I can tell you are a man who won't talk this through. I also know you won't relent."

Trent deliberately handed Mitch his rope.

"Have the first punch," taunted Brandt. "Hero, here's the only warning I'm going to say. Make it a good one. If I get up, you won't."

From the pit of his stomach, Brandt made a sharp laugh. His kick came first, followed by a punch. Trent easily blocked both of them. Trent stepped up, punching Brandt in the chin. As he fell to the ground unconscious, Trent tied him up, using his belt. Eventually Brandt opened his eyes. He glared up at his warden.

"You might be great at Judo, I'm a champion rodeo rider. I'm the fastest hog tier in Australia."

Andy slapped Trent on the back. "What can I say? I've fifty bucks on you today. You better win, or I'll chase your arse all over Australia for your hide."

"Your winnings are already in the bag, big fella."

Mitch collected Kaite from Andy's small office and joined Naomi and Trent.

"The sheriff is on his way over," announced Kaite. "I found him walking around when Brandt wanted to fight."

The friendly cop marched up to the group and handcuffed Brandt, forcing him to stand.

"My right-hand man has tracked the other two. One is a hired pilot. He has no idea what transpired here. The female, it turns out, is Brandt's girlfriend, or should I say, and I quote from her mouth, 'ex-girlfriend!'" The cop shook Trent's hand. He shoved Brandt in the shoulder to signal he needed to walk towards the police car.

"Is everyone okay?" yelled Earl Stanton, sprinting down the boulevard towards the group. He abruptly stopped when he saw everyone laughing. "You kids are all jokers." Casually swatting his hand through the air, he walked off towards the under-fifteen's bull riding event.

CHAPTER EIGHTEEN

NAOMI SLIPPED her arm around the waist of her hero. "Thanks for coming to my rescue."

"Not a problem. City blokes think, suburban. Out here in the middle of Australia, a man has to think differently."

"What would you do if Brandt came from the country?"

"I'd still win. The only difference; the fight might have lasted a bit longer." Trent winked at Naomi's startled expression. "I've one more ride."

"I thought when you won the ride on the bull the day was over," stated Naomi.

"The day has only just started warming up," answered Trent.

"He wins every event he enters each year, don't you brother?" said Mitch. "Mark my words, one of these days I'm going to beat you. I'm not far behind you in the bull ride."

Trent slapped his brother on the shoulder. "When you get a little stronger, you'll give me a run for the money."

Mitch scooped Kaite up into his arms. "My wrestling match is in fifteen minutes. Do you think I'll win?" he probed.

"Yes, I do," said Trent.

"You two are typical brothers," giggled Naomi.

"We'll catch up when I'm holding the wrestling trophy." With Kaite in his arms, Mitch sprinted towards the sign-in tent.

Trent placed his hands on Naomi's hips. After kissing her, he displayed a scolded expression. "This time, don't run off."

"I'm not going anywhere!" she exclaimed.

"You said the same thing half an hour ago."

"This time, I mean it."

Naomi climbed the fence ready to watch the next contest. Trent jumped, clinging to the top railing. Leaning gently against Naomi's shoulder, he pointed to a fit man wearing an oversized wide brimmed hat. He sat heavy on a white thoroughbred horse. Both looked a little anxious.

"He's my opposition," explained Trent. "He's an expert at roping a cow. Quick too. He warned me a month ago I should be practicing. He informed me today I'm going to lose."

The man stared at Trent. He touched the brim of his hat. Trent did the same. Naomi surmised the gesture to be only a friendly bush rivalry signal.

A buzzer sounded. The crowd roared. It took eight seconds for the contest to end.

"That was one quick contest," yelled Naomi, over the cheers and the clapping of the crowd.

"To remain champ, I have to rope a cow and hog tie it in seven seconds," said Trent.

"It sounds impossible."

"It's in the bag."

Trent jumped from the fence, marched across the arena, waving to the cheering crowd. He blew Naomi a kiss and climbed on to his horse. While waiting for the start, he patted the horse's neck. He leaned forward whispering something in its ear. He sat straight and glanced at Naomi.

Trent nodded at the Judge who held the car horn. When the crowd hushed the man pushed a green button. The wooden gates swung open. The one-year-old calf sprinted off for freedom. Trent and his horse came up from behind. Unclipping the rope, Trent started swinging the loop above his head in a second and a half. Trent downed the cow, hog-tying it in a clean six and a half seconds.

Naomi stared at the timekeeper who appeared to be shaking his head in disbelief.

"Ladies and gentlemen," he called slowly through the megaphone. "Today you have witnessed history in the making. Trent Stanton has shattered the time he set last year. He has again shown everyone here today why he's still champion. Put your hands together for Trent and a new record."

The crowd cheered which included a standing ovation. A Mexican wave erupted, circling the arena three times.

The man Trent defeated walked over, extending his hand. They clasped each other's hands making the handshake look to be a little strained. Both stared at each other. Neither of the men seemed to want to be the first to look away.

"Congratulations on a fine ride."

"Thanks, Tom," said Trent.

"Here's a friendly warning; wait for next year."

"I'm looking forward to it."

Another Mexican wave started up, moving around the fenced arena, interrupting the standoff. Both men looked at the crowd at the same time. There were hoots, cheers, yelling and clapping.

Tom spat in the sawdust. "Don't forget what I told you."

Trent stood his ground watching Tom walk off, dusting the bottom of his boots as he went.

A middle-aged man wearing a black suit and a white open neck shirt looked official as he marched to the center of the oval, tapping a microphone with his left hand. "Everyone, please, a little quiet."

A whisper quiet quickly descended on the arena. The eyes of every spectator stared at the Judge.

"I want to take this opportunity to congratulate Trent Stanton on a wonderful exhibition today. Everyone, please give this champion another round of applause as he comes to collect his trophy."

Mitch slipped Trent a small box as he started to walk towards the middle of the arena. Trent waved to the onlookers who immediately cheered louder.

"Speech, speech, speech," chorused the crowd.

Trent snatched up the microphone and pushed his hand into the air. A young girl in tight blue jeans and a white singlet walked over and presented the huge trophy of a gold-plated cow mounted on a mahogany-colored board. She craned her neck and kissed Trent on the cheek.

"Congratulations. When you're ready to take me on a date give me a call."

"Lucky gal," yelled a middle-aged woman standing next to Naomi and Kaite.

Naomi flashed her a cold icy stare.

The woman leaned sideways. "Lucky girl who corners Trent," she whispered. "If he doesn't hurry up and choose a wife, I'm going to insist he picks me even if it's a shotgun wedding." She stuck her hand out for an outback handshake. "Name's Vie. It's short for Violetta."

"Naomi," she replied, shaking the woman's hand.

Kaite leaned close, whispering in Naomi's ear. "What I've seen of the outback, I've decided to leave the city. The Oasis is where I want to spend the remainder of my life."

Naomi felt the heavy burden magically lift from off her shoulders. Maybe, just maybe her fantasies might come true after all. Only one hurdle remained, and she doubted whether Trent could ever discover the perfect gift. How could he, out here in the middle of Australia where education is low? Again, she tried to decide on what to do.

"Kaite, what do you think of Mitch?"

"He's a hunk and a half. He sure knows how to push the right buttons."

"Have you talked to Mitch about wanting to stay?"

Kaite pushed the sides of her hair up using her hands. "What do you think?"

"He asked you to marry him?" quizzed Naomi. Her gaze zeroed in on the diamond ring she wore on the finger of her left hand.

"You bet he did."

"When?" questioned Naomi.

"He asked me before we stood on the hill looking at the cows."

"So now I know the meaning of the wrestle?"

"Yes. Mitch explained to Trent what he'd planned. They were both excited. Their little brotherly talk ended in a family wrestle."

"Congratulations. You deserve it. Mitch is a good bloke."

Naomi switched her attention back to the arena so she could feast her eyes on Trent.

"I'd like to name a few people who need thanking," bellowed Trent through the microphone. "First, I want to thank the organizers of today and to everyone who has made this annual day spectacular. Twenty years is no mean feat. I love to make a special mention of a wonderful lady. I've explained to her I don't waste words. For the first time, I need to say what's on my mind. Everyone, please give a warm welcome to the most wonderful lady I know. Naomi Fitzgerald, please come out."

Naomi's face flushed bright red. Her eyes widened in fear.

Vie leaned sideways. "I believe Trent's calling you little darlin', get out there."

"How did you guess?"

"I didn't, you just told me. Besides, you're a pretty little thing. Take no offence when I say you smell like a city chick."

Naomi frowned, smelling her clothes.

"Don't worry about the smell. One day the country air has a way of changing the smell of city folk. I know what I'm talking about."

"If what you say is true, the only way you'd know is if you came from the city. To me, you look like you've never been there."

Vie nodded at Naomi then she winked. "Trent's a waitin'."

"Thank you for being so friendly." Naomi clasped both hands on the top of the wooden railing, heaving her body up and over the fence. Slowly she climbed down the other side. She found Vie smiling at her.

"You'll change. A few years out here, no one will ever know you came from the city," she whispered.

Naomi pushed her head through the gap in the wooden railings. "How long since you've seen the city?"

"A wonderful twenty years."

Naomi straightened her clothes. She kept her gaze glued on Trent as she walked.

"Slow and steady," she mumbled under her breath. "I certainly don't want to embarrass myself further by falling face first into the sawdust."

The crowd cheered her on. Naomi felt a warm feeling shoot through her body from her feet to the top of her head. She felt more special than ever. She waved at the crowd which made the people cheer louder.

Trent put his arm around Naomi's waist before speaking into the microphone. Three hundred people listened to his every word.

"Naomi, we haven't known each other long," he started.

"What are you up to?" she whispered, appearing slightly puzzled.

"Keep it moving," yelled Earl Stanton from somewhere over Naomi's left shoulder.

Looking at the crowd, Trent continued. "Andy, thanks for the information big fella on this so called, 'perfect gift.' I have to disagree about your theory it has to be a puppy."

The crowd immediately roared laughing.

Naomi whispered a nervous giggle. Had this cowboy successfully discovered what she called the perfect gift? "Please don't say," she managed to mumble. "It's not important."

Trent either didn't hear her, or he ignored what she said.

"Naomi Fitzgerald, I believe I have discovered the meaning of the perfect gift."

Naomi mouthed the word 'don't.'

"'The,' means the man. The word gift represents something small; important in a girl's life."

"Go Trent."

The yell deep amongst the sea of onlookers sent the crowd into a whispered frenzy. The entire gathering glared at Andy to keep quiet.

Trent placed the microphone under his arm. Downing his left knee, he looked up at Naomi. He reached out, taking hold of her left hand. Using his free hand, he produced a small red box.

The entire crowd instantly hushed. Even the cows stopped moving.

"Naomi, there is only one thing missing in my life. My dreams will be made into reality if you would please seriously consider accepting my proposal to be my wife." He slowly stood. "Before you answer, I believe there is one word yet to be discovered."

Naomi started to tremble. Her knees turned from jelly to water. She couldn't understand why she didn't crumble to the ground. She wanted to feel Trent's magic rope tighten about her waist so she could be pulled towards his strong, safe arms.

Trent's voice broke through her fuzzy thoughts.

"The middle word of the secret line means you are looking for a man who will surrender his whole heart to just one lady. Naomi, if you'd accept my proposal of marriage my whole heart belongs to you."

CHAPTER NINETEEN

THE PRIEST looked up at the small congregation. Naomi stood square to Trent at the altar. Her white silk and lace wedding dress looked picture-perfect. The atmosphere in the church felt overwhelming.

Naomi flashed Kaite a satisfied expression. Glancing around the small beautiful old chapel, built decades earlier in one corner of the Oasis, Naomi looked out of the small plain glass window at the blue sky. Her eyes widened in disbelief when she saw a leaf fall from the large apple tree. She squealed. Tears streamed down Naomi's face as she ran past the astonished family members on her way out into the sunlight. She sprinted to where the leaf floated to the ground. Naomi knelt on the carpet style grass.

Trent sprinted to her side. "Naomi, what's happened?"

"I can't marry you. I'm so sorry." She lowered her head further to the ground, sobbing uncontrollably. Her entire body trembled underneath her wedding dress.

"I don't understand. I thought you and I were the happiest couple on the planet? You said those words to me only last night when we walked in the dark holding hands while watching the moon slowly rise."

"I am, at least I thought I was."

"Naomi, please look at me. Whatever has caused you this pain you're going through, I'm here to help?"

"I saw a falling leaf. It's a bad omen from years ago. Now it has happened again."

With his hand, Trent gently cupped Naomi's chin and lifted her head. He kissed her forehead. He looked at her water-soaked eyes. He didn't joke or say anything to put her down. Instead, his words were honey smooth. "A leaf, that falls off a tree signals it is autumn. In

America, they call it the fall. A falling leaf has no other significance than to help the tree to grow."

Naomi slowly relayed the story of Bill and his bigamist ways and how much he deeply hurt her. Every autumn, no matter how hard she tried to forget the haunting thoughts of her disastrous wedding day, the vivid, painful memories came flooding back. She had been totally devastated by his lies. His deceitfulness caused her heart to be torn in two.

Trent lifted his bride off the ground. He palmed his hand at the Oasis.

"This is your home now. You belong here. Today is the first day of a new season. It also signals a new life for the both of us. I will be by your side every day for the remainder of our years. You have no need to fear anything from your past. Come, let us begin our journey."

"Thank you for your kind thoughtful words," whispered Naomi.

Trent placed her gently on the ground. He stooped, picking up two leaves from off the ground. He handed one to Naomi, the other he held.

"When I look at these leaves, I see a brand-new season is not far away. I know winter will be first, but spring is just around the corner."

Naomi turned the brown leaf over in her hand.

"See," whispered Trent. "It's only a leaf. It came from the tree you're standing under. It decomposes which helps the tree to grow." Trent scrunched the dry leaf in his hand and let the flakes fall to the ground.

He nodded.

Naomi scrunched her leaf, opened her hand and watched the flakes she created fall about her feet.

"From this moment forth, I Naomi will never let the bad memories of years gone by upset me again."

Trent kissed his bride.

"Take me back into the church; it's time we were married."

The wedding ceremony successfully came to the finale. The priest who'd been flown out to the Oasis for the special occasion seemed pleased.

Trent looked longingly at Naomi. His eyes weren't hiding the inner man anymore.

"You're the most beautiful person I've ever met. I promise to love and cherish you from this moment forward. Even after death, I will love you."

"I Naomi will love and cherish you Trent Stanton until the day I die and beyond."

"I now pronounce you husband and wife," announced the priest.

He radiated a proud look as Trent and Naomi kissed for the first time since being married.

To the cheering of the small group, Trent escorted Naomi from the cottage style church in one corner of the Oasis to the lush green lawn where a white marquee had been set up ready for the wedding reception. Every flower appeared to be in full color. The sun quickly warmed the air. The sparkling river had slowed to a crawl. It looked inviting even to Naomi. The Oasis could not have looked any more spectacular. The wedding photos were taken and the reception appeared to be in full swing.

In the trees, the birds were singing their love song. Naomi felt a brand-new life had been laid out before her, one she only ever dreamt about. She felt a warm tingling sensation travel throughout her body. In a strange way, she wanted her life to speed along so she could read about her exciting adventures she had with Trent by her side. Naomi looked forward to the years which were to come. She turned away from the crowd of single women and got ready to throw the bridal bouquet high over her shoulders.

Kaite leapt over the top of several young ladies, grabbing the bouquet of flowers in full flight. She stood triumphant looking at

Mitch. He sprinted to her side, scooped her up one handed and carried her to a vacant chair.

"Trent, does the scene remind you of anything?" asked Naomi, laughing.

He scooped her up, white-lace wedding dress, silk train and all. "I've taught my brother everything I know."

"It seems another wedding is blowing in from the north sooner than expected," chirped Naomi.

"It'll have to wait until we get back from our honeymoon."

"You haven't let a syllable of a single word escape your mouth on where you intend to take me," scolded Naomi. "You really should say."

"It's a big surprise," said Trent. "After all, I need to have a least one secret left."

EPILOGUE

JAKE GENTLY closed the leather-bound book. With tears in his eyes, he stared at his sister. The old man who resembled a street bum opened the door to the tiny room. He walked in, stone-faced, straight and tall. A tightly coiled length of rope hung from his huge brass belt buckle. The tall, slender lady who walked into the room, last, closed the door. She walked over and gripped Jake's arm. Her smile seemed warm, friendly and looked natural like a country girl. Anyone could tell the couple belonged together. The lady nodded at her daughter.

Bernice, sitting at the mahogany desk next to Jake, stood.

Jake seemed reluctant to stand. Bernice saw to it he did.

"Mother," he whimpered in a ghostly whisper. "I thought you were dead. I saw you lying in the coffin. I came here today to give my last respects. Why the fake funeral? If you wanted to talk, you could have rung me. You didn't have to go through such an exuberant hoax."

Trent and Naomi squared themselves to their son.

"I suppose you're expecting an apology from us for forcing you to come here under false pretenses?" probed Naomi.

"It'll be a good start."

"I'm not at liberty to give one," gushed Naomi. Her voice still sounded warm, yet she spoke in a firm tone. "The funeral just happened to be a ploy to convince you, Jake dear, you should come home."

"Son, you know I don't talk unless I have something to say."

"Father, speak your mind. I know I have never listened to a single word you have said in the past, however, after reading the leather-bound book about you and mother's life, I fully regret my decision. I've been a fool every day since I turned away from you and the Oasis and headed for the city."

"Say no more," insisted Trent, lifting his hand in the air. "What's done, has been swept away by the river that flows into the underground tunnel back at the Oasis. You need to make a choice about your future. A wise decision is preferred."

"The Bible explains about the prodigal son. He left, wised up and went home. I feel the same way," whispered Jake, interrupting.

"On behalf of your mother, I thank you for reading her memoirs," said Trent.

"I never knew the turmoil, you, and she went through."

"Now you do."

"I need to thank you for conceiving this plan to persuade our son to come home," said Naomi. She kissed Trent on the cheek.

"Naomi, I only thought of the idea. If you didn't lie motionless in the coffin, Jake might never have read the book." Trent switched his gaze to Bernice. "I want to thank you for putting so many important memories down in writing."

"Dad, Mum, it had been worth every hour just to see my brother one more time."

"I didn't know mum could ever be so dedicated to the Oasis, or to you, father. What a transformation. I'd never have picked my mother for a city chick," moaned Jake.

The group chuckled, slapping each other on the shoulder.

"You should have stuck around?" snarled Bernice.

"I thought if I stayed out there in the middle of Australia, I'd be bored. I longed for the city, the people, the bright lights, and the nightlife," admitted Jake.

"I never did have a boring day in my entire life. As for the city and the night life, I've tasted it. I came sprinting back to the safety of the Oasis," explained Bernice.

"I never dreamt the city isn't what I thought it would be," whispered Jake, starting to pull at the edge of the leather-bound book.

"You should have asked me about the city. There's no comparison between it and the Oasis. One has a fast pace which can have an exciting life, however, at every corner, there is a danger. The other has a relaxed, peaceful life, which is adventurous yet safe," stated Naomi.

"Son, let's go home," said Trent.

"Only if we go to live at the Oasis. I want to hear more stories," stammered Jake, sliding the leather-bound book off the table. Holding it tight against his chest, he walked towards the door. He turned towards the group.

"Coming?"

Dear reader,

Thank you for reading my novel 'The perfect gift.' I do hope you enjoyed it. Any feedback is gratefully accepted. The information you, the reader give, helps me to become a more professional author.

My novels are based on the Australian culture. Some of the spelling is Australian. Thanks for your understanding.

Again, thank you for your support, for without you, the reader, I wouldn't have anyone to read my work.

Mark Stewart

ABOUT THE AUTHOR

Mark Stewart is an inspirational author.

The transformation from when I started to edit his work until now has been amazing. His hard work and dedication have helped him to write more professionally.

Mark is undeniably the one to watch.

Mathew Lang

Mark Stewart is an acclaimed author.

He loves to write fiction right across the board from romance adventure

to crime and onwards to science fiction and children's books.

His fast-paced novels will keep you on the edge of your seat from the first word to the last.

Mark lives in Melbourne Australia and tries to

keep to the Aussie lingo and customs.

Rosemary Cantala

Other novels by Mark Stewart:
Kiss on the bridge.
Kiss on the bridge two.
Kiss on the bridge three.
Don't tell my secret.
201 May Street
The girl from Emerald Hill
Ladies' Club
Mistress
Book of secrets
The perfect gift:
Legendary blue diamond.
Legendary blue diamond two
Legendary blue diamond three.
The Blood Red Rose.
Blood red Rose Two.
Blood red Rose Thee.
Planet X91 series
Fire Games.
Heart of a spider.
I know your secret.

About the Author

Mark Stewart is an acclaimed author.

He loves to write fiction right across the board from romance adventure

to crime and onwards to science fiction and children's books.

His fast-paced novels will keep you on the edge of your seat from the first word to the last.

Mark lives in Melbourne Australia and tries to keep to the Aussie lingo and customs.